MW01127607

VOODOO KISS
Ancient Legends

JAYDE SCOTT

Other titles in the Ancient Legends series

A Job From Hell
Doomed
Bewitched

Other titles by Jayde Scott

Black Wood
Mortal Star
The Divorce Club
Born to Spy

©Copyright 2012 Jayde Scott
The right of Jayde Scott to be identified as the author of this work
has been asserted in accordance with the Copyright, Designs and Patents Act
1988.

All rights reserved. No part of this publication may be reproduced,
stored in a retrieval system, or transmitted in any form or by any means,
electronic, mechanical, photocopying, recording or otherwise, without the
prior permission of the author.

This is a work of fiction and any resemblance between the
characters and persons living or dead is purely coincidental.

All rights reserved.
ISBN: 1470055759
ISBN-13: 978-1470055752

For Foxy, Silver and Tabby

You taught me the true meaning of love …

Acknowledgments

I'd like to thank my beloved spouse for the inspiration and for the immense support. You're my rock, and I couldn't have done it without you. A huge thank you to my new editor, Shannon, for the invaluable insight and for being so thorough. Thank you to fellow author, Christine Peebles, for taking the time to critique this novel.

And, last but not least, a huge thanks to all my wonderful readers. I hope you'll enjoy reading this book as much as I enjoyed writing it.

Fools rush in where angels fear to tread
The Fallen will cheer
Where the Gifted mend the dead

- Jayde Scott

Prologue

1678

He came after the fall of darkness when all was quiet and the relentless heat of the late August sun had long waned into a freezing night. I wrapped my shawl around my aching bones and opened the door to let him in, but he just lingered in the doorway, his black hood covering most of his pale face, smooth as marble, and shiny black eyes.

"Esmeralda."

For a moment, my breath caught in my throat. The time had finally come, meaning there was no going back now. I shouldn't be scared. After all, it had been my decision to call for him. I had no choice than to go through with it because Death was already lurking in the shadows.

A breeze blew across my face; the cool air felt good on my hot-burning skin. I hoped against all odds I wouldn't pass out before the deal was sealed. It was time to hurry so I pointed behind me. Without my invitation he would never be able to cross the threshold. "Come on in, Warrior."

He bowed before me and stepped past into the dimly lit hut with dried lavender hanging from strings attached across the ceiling, his boots barely making any sound on the naked ground that hadn't received a good scrub ever since the fever got hold of me.

"Over here." I pulled a chair for him when white spots filled my vision and I collapsed into a heap on the cold floor.

His piercing eyes met my gaze. "Time is running out for you."

"You think I don't know that?" Laughing bitterly, I scrambled to my feet and pointed at the chair. He nodded but didn't take me up on the offer. Instead, he marched over to the hearth with the burning logs and pulled out a scroll from under his coat, then handed it to me.

My eyes scanned the handwriting, soaking up the beauty of the cursive and the words I had never learned to read.

"Is the agreement not to your liking?" the warrior asked.

"All is well." Drawing a deep breath I grabbed the dagger from his outstretched hand and pierced its tip into my thumb, letting two drops of blood stain the paper. "Then it is done?"

"Not yet. Reincarnation requires personal sacrifice." He pushed the scroll back under his cloak and removed the hood. I stared at the pale skin covering high cheekbones and the unnaturally black eyes, dark as puddles, soaking up the light in the room. He seemed young, maybe eighteen summers old, and yet I knew it couldn't be. His race would only send a master to deal with my proposition.

"You will inherit this sacred land and all the souls I have bound to it throughout the years. I have fulfilled my part of the bargain, now it's your turn." My voice shook because his eerie eyes made me nervous. I hid my wringing hands behind my back.

The warrior inched closer, his gaze prodding into mine. "And so we shall. As agreed, you, Esmeralda, Priestess of the Seventh Order, will be reborn as the seventh daughter of the seventh daughter of the Romanov dynasty. Your powers shall know no boundaries for they were bestowed to you by the Goddess herself."

I nodded. "Yes, that was part of the agreement."

He held up a hand to stop me. "There is more, however. As we grant life, we're also owners to take it. Nothing but the Blade of Sorrow will be able to kill you. Once it does, your skills will pass onto the owner of the blade and your soul will be forever bound to the Cemetery of the Dead."

"No." I shook my head vigorously. "That wasn't part of my offer. I will not agree to it."

"It's too late. See your mark?" He pulled out the scroll and unrolled it. I peered mortified at the blood soaking the paper, dripping onto the ground. A sudden flash of light blinded my eyes. I blinked and returned my focus to the contract. The blood formed a perfect hexagon across the entire scroll. I couldn't help but gasp. The warrior continued, "The goddess has accepted your sacrifice."

Outside, a strong wind began to howl through the nearby trees, rattling the windowpanes. The warrior started to whisper in a language I didn't understand. A sharp pain, like that of a knife, pierced my heart and I dropped to my knees, clutching the rags I had worn for more years than I could count. My breathing came in labored heaps, but my mind remained surprisingly sharp.

The door opened with a creak and he flew in, his great wings flapping softly. The reaper—a creature of Heaven and Hell who lingered around me for many months, waiting for me to draw my last breath so he could transport my soul wherever he was meant to take it. He stood directly before me—seven feet tall with a surprisingly human face. Its dark gaze sharpened on me as he let out a piercing scream coming straight from the pit of hell. It was the first time I got a good look at the creature, all skin as dark as coal and eyes as deep as the ocean.

I turned my head to look at the chanting warrior, begging him to save me, but he averted his gaze. On my knees, I pulled myself to the far side of the wall where a stack of hay covered by a thin sheet served as my sleeping chamber. The reaper lurched, his enormous wings fluttering behind him. Sharp claws cut into my chest, the pain intensifying until I could no longer breathe. I knew then that I was about to die.

My scream found its way out of my throat a moment before my vision blurred and the room became darkness. What would be the purpose in fighting with a body wrecked from age and disease? I sighed, ready to succumb to my fate. Instead of fighting, I let go willingly.

I had been deceived by the ones I had trusted.

Chapter 1

Present day New York City

My *babushka* had been a witch. And while she couldn't do more than the usual love potion and heal the odd sore throat, she had always insisted I was a witch too, though nowhere near embracing my powers. Not before people didn't come for me to ask me to fulfill a very important task. While her superstitious words had always made me laugh, they had also left a strange foreboding feeling in the pit of my stomach. I had always been one to believe in ghosts and things that go bump in the night, so when my life started to take a strange turn, I couldn't help but admit that something *paranormal* was going on and that my grandmother had been right. How else could I explain the bizarre events happening recently?

Ever since a few weeks ago when the TV set switched itself on to a show with a red-haired girl and her pretty, plump friend calling herself a psychic or something, my life hadn't been the same again. They claimed to have a message from someone by the name of Theo. My half sister's name was Theo. She was murdered a while back. I could tell myself that particular occurrence was a mere coincidence, but a few other things I couldn't explain. Starting with the black crow that I swear had been following me for the last month, always cawing on my windowsill at night, to the pitch black I kept seeing in my dreams. It was always a black abyss that beckoned to me, drawing me in and keeping me paralyzed, until I woke up with a jolt, drenched in sweat and too perturbed to get back to sleep.

I'd been so sleep deprived and anxious I almost failed my college admission exam that was supposed to get me into drama school. Hoping the summer vacation would help me get my crap together, I agreed to a one-week vacation to Brazil. Granted, it was more of a proposition from my boyfriend, Gael, but I was thankful for the opportunity when he surprised me with two flight tickets to Rio de Janeiro. My bags were packed and cluttered the tiny hall to my apartment now. My best friend, Cindy, promised to feed my fish and water my plants. It was the trip of a lifetime, not least because Gael was talking about taking our relationship to the next level now that I was about to start college. So why was I hesitating?

Standing on the stage of Area 9 with a guitar cradled in my arms and a microphone in front of me, I sang the last words to *Harried*. Even though my mind was a million miles away, my voice rose and fell to the bittersweet melody, my hands sliding up and down the guitar neck the way they had done countless times before. The last tune echoed through the large bar.

"Well done, Soph," my band mate, Aaron, said.

The few people seated near the edge, frat boys and their dates plus the usual drunks, clapped half-heartedly. I muttered a thank you and goodnight to the crowd even though I knew no one was listening, and made my way out through the back entrance, inhaling the putrid smell of garbage cans and piss.

I leaned against the dirty wall facing the door and fished for the cigarette pack stashed inside the back pocket of my tiny leather skirt, then lit one, inhaling deeply. The smoke made me cough once or twice before my throat settled and the burning sensation in my eyes subsided. I had been smoking long before my sister died, but I still couldn't get used to it. As if my body protested against the slow poison destroying it from the inside. Or maybe Theo, who had never liked my habit, kept protesting from the otherworld, influencing my unconscious. Either way, I took a final deep drag before tossing it on the ground and stomping on the burning tip, feeling depressed and disgusted with myself for no apparent reason.

The cool air blew my hair into my face. Wings flapped to my right, the sound making me flinch. Pressing my palm against my racing heart, I peered into the darkness stretching behind the garbage cans, almost expecting the irritating crow to stare back at me. But nothing moved.

"Silly," I muttered, feeling even sillier for talking to myself. Nothing a good night's sleep couldn't fix, if only I'd finally get one.

I walked back to the entrance and grabbed the doorknob when my hand froze. Someone was behind me. The smell of musk, candles and herbs invaded my nostrils. I could feel someone's hot breath on my exposed neck. My pulse accelerated, my mind stopped working. For a moment, I just stood there devoid of any thoughts before I turned to face him.

"You all right?" His voice came low and deep but he sounded young. Maybe twenty or twenty-five. A dark hood hung over his forehead and partially obscured his features. I squinted trying to get a closer look, but the lamp over the entrance door didn't give enough light.

"You want in?" I nodded and stepped aside to let him into the club, but when I turned my head he disappeared right before my eyes.

I peered to the left and right, wondering where he'd gone, or whether my imagination was running wild. A few sleepless nights and two painkillers could sure enough make one imagine things. Unless he could sprint ten feet to reach the corner in two seconds, he couldn't have been there because the alleyway had been empty when I stepped out of the club, and it sure was empty now.

No, my mind had played a trick on me. It tended to do that a lot lately, particularly after Theo's death. Inhaling the freezing night air, I wrapped my arms

15

around me to stop me from shivering and counted to ten, then left.

When I returned to the tiny room behind the stage, my band mate slash rookie, manager and everything else, Aaron, had packed away my guitar and was now loading our equipment into the van. Most clubs had an amplifier, speakers and microphone for the odd karaoke night, but as semi-professionals we prided ourselves on using our own stuff, even if we could barely afford paying the rental fee on the van.

"Want me to drive you home?" Aaron asked from the driver's seat. I shook my head as I regarded his spiky green hair and the ring piercing his lower lip. He looked more like a punk than a rocker. Then again, Aaron had never been one to fit into a group, stereotype or otherwise.

"Suit yourself," he said and started the engine. I watched him speed off in the distance, then returned to the bar to call myself a taxi. As much as I would've wanted to take him up on the offer, because I really couldn't afford another taxi drive home, I knew it was for the best. Better to avoid another jealousy fueled fight with Gael before we even started our first vacation together.

The taxi ride home to my tiny apartment in Brooklyn took about fifteen minutes, which I spent leaning my head against the cold glass as I watched my distorted face in the car window. The street lights illuminated my recently dyed jet black hair and

16

emphasizing the dark shadows under my eyes. Gael had said he preferred my ash blonde hair. His superficial statement enraged me. But even if I wanted to please him, which I didn't, my natural hair color reminded me too much of my sister, so I had to do something about it. As a rock chick, it was either black or burgundy. I figured, black was the more reasonable choice. It made me look as haunted as I felt inside.

The car finally stopped. I paid and thanked the driver, then entered the dilapidated building and rode the elevator up to the seventh floor. My roommate wasn't here for the week, which suited me just fine. I had been having a hard time explaining the crow perched on my windowsill day in, day out. I took a few steps toward the window to shoo it away, then stopped, changing my mind because I was too tired to bother. Instead, I skimmed quickly through my evening routine and then dropped onto my bed, unable to sleep for a long time because of the cawing outside.

***

Less than five hours later, after yet another sleepless night, the piercing ring of the bell interrupted my trail of thoughts trying to recall whether I had remembered everything. The noise didn't stop, signaling my visitor was slowly losing their patience, so I tossed my sticky list on the breakfast table and hurried to open.

Gael, dressed in his usual white shirt and brown slacks, stood in the doorway, his mouth curved into a lazy smile, the faintest scent of sandalwood wafting from him. I reached for him and he pulled me into a tight embrace, his lips locking with mine in a brief, sloppy kiss.

"Ready?" His dark eyes sparkled with anticipation as he ran a hand through his light brown hair that was a tad too long to soften his square jaw and strong features.

Not really. Sleep deprived as I was, I felt like crap and yet I couldn't show him. Gael didn't like me complaining. "Yep." I pulled him after me into the apartment and closed the door behind us, my nerves flaring up again. The strange feeling in the pit of my stomach hadn't subsided ever since Gael had presented the flight tickets, but I associated it with the fact that my love life was moving way too fast in a direction I wasn't ready to take just yet. The pain of losing Theo was as strong as on that fateful day when I heard of her death. The wound in my heart still burned too bright to let me focus on a relationship. In fact, I had been considering breaking off with him for a few weeks now. He was hot, no doubt about that, but the spark just wasn't really there.

"Is that all?" Gael pointed at the two worn suitcases in the corner. The brown leather was torn in places, a string was bound around the grip in case the old buckle might give in. I nodded shyly, embarrassed that I couldn't afford at least some decent looking second hand suitcase, let alone a brand name. Gael O'Connor originated from a long line of Irish aristocrats with plenty of money to his name, but if my lack of finances bothered him, he didn't show it. In one swift movement, he lifted my suitcases and carried them down the seven stories to the waiting taxi. I locked the door and followed behind, the uneasy sensation in the pit of my stomach intensifying and my thoughts running wild. Did I feel uneasy because I had never been a fan of traveling? Did I feel guilty because I felt I should be grieving instead of enjoying my life? Partly I hoped and prayed Theo's death was a huge misunderstanding, meaning she might just come back and I wouldn't be here. I knew all the obsessing was nonsense, but I couldn't help myself. Trying to push the nagging thoughts to the back of my mind, I snuggled against Gael, who wrapped his arm around me.

We arrived at JFK International Airport with half an hour to spare during which we grabbed a cup of coffee and made our way to the gate. It was still early on a foggy September Monday but already huge crowds of travelers had gathered at every corner, chattering as though they enjoyed every minute of their journey. Most travelers were well dressed which was something I adored about NY. Everyone was so fashionable in a casual way, reminding me a bit of France where fashion was everything.

I wiped my damp hands on my jean skirt and peered at Gael from the corner of my eye, admiring his strong features and the way he always seemed to look presentable whereas I always looked like a hot mess with my jeans and chipped nail polish.

"Nervous?" he asked with a grin. I nodded even though I knew better than to wear my feelings on my sleeve. He might be able to catch a glimpse of my fear, but he had no idea of the hurricane tormenting my stomach. Boarding a plane had always been one of my many phobias ever since I took my first ten-hour flight from Moscow to NY, which I spent bowled over the matchbox toilet. I could only hope I had grown out of that habit, but it didn't seem like it.

Gael grabbed my arm and pulled me against his chest whispering, "There's nothing to be nervous about, Soph." His warm breath, smelling of fresh coffee with the slightest hint of mint, caressed my cheek. I sighed and leaned against his broad chest, inhaling his aftershave I had grown to love during the six months we had been dating.

Six months. That's a long time for a nineteen-year-old. A lot can happen in six months. One can finally graduate from school, move out of the motherly abode and seek to get a job to support one's music career. Or make friends, go partying, enjoy youth. My cheeks started to burn. Really, I was such a moron to have the thoughts I had when my boyfriend couldn't be more caring and supportive. But it wasn't my fault I saw him more as a friend than a lover.

"You never told me how the gig was," Gael said, as though reading my mind. I raised my gaze to meet his dark eyes.

"Great but I might as well have mimed naked on stage."

He smiled. "Now *that* would've definitely grabbed their attention."

"Everyone was so drunk I doubt they'd have noticed the difference."

"Everybody has to start somewhere. You'll be a star soon enough." He always said that which is why I had learned to stop complaining. If he believed in me then I might as well start believing too.

"Why Rio?" I asked, changing the subject.

"What?"

I moistened my lips. "You never told me why you're taking me to Brazil."

Gael averted his gaze, his eyes glazing over for a moment telling me he was considering his answer. Even though we had only been dating for six months, I had known him and his family for a few years, long before my sister died and his brother was killed around the same time. While I was still dreaming about Theo daily Gael seemed to barely remember Derrick's name.

"It's a beautiful city...for lovers," he said eventually.

"Been there before?" I marveled at how I wasn't even jealous that he had brought other girls on his vacations.

He shrugged. "A few times."

21

I laughed, feeling the uneasiness in the pit of my stomach again. "Care to elaborate?"

"There isn't much to say about it."

His lips curled into a grin, but I could say from the strange twinkle in his eyes that he was hiding something. I nudged him playfully. "Ah, I like your style. So you take a chick down there, get her all drunk on samba so you can hook up with her. Not bad. If I were a guy with money I might just do the same. Not."

He laughed as he pulled me closer. "There weren't any other girls. Just me and my family on a boring, private beach." He pointed behind me. "Let's board."

I nodded and followed him through the usual boarding motions. A flight attendant accompanied us inside the aircraft.

"Take a seat. I'll be right back," Gael said.

Shrugging, I did as he instructed, surprised to find Gael had booked us first class seats with all the extra perks. Then again, what did I expect? That he fly economy like every other normal human being? As I took my window seat with the extra legroom, I watched him talk with the stewardess, his voice too low to hear, his hand hovering in mid-air mere inches away from her arm. I turned away, slightly irritated with myself that I wasn't feeling the jealousy I thought I should feel.

Gael returned to his seat with a glass of water, which I drank hastily. "Ready for the trip of your life?" he asked, grabbing my hand.

22

"Looking forward to it." I smiled and touched his hand, then leaned back, comfortable. My eyes felt heavy after the lack of sleep from last night. I slumped into my seat and let myself drift into an uneasy nap accompanied by the sound of fluttering wings inside my head.

Chapter 2

I slept through most of the flight. By the time we were ready to land in Rio de Janeiro, my spirits had lifted and I even felt excited to visit one of the most remarkable cities in the world. Granted, it did have a reputation for mugging and kidnapping, but with Gael by my side I felt ready to capture the world.

"Sorry about this morning," I said as we squeezed our way through the huge crowd gathering at customs.

"No worries," Gael whispered. "Just make sure you clutch your handbag tight."

My handbag wasn't the only thing I'd clutch tight. I peered at the tall, tanned girls with their generous cleavages ready on display for anyone who wanted a second look. My hand moved to Gael's, squeezing his until he shot me an amused look. I smiled back out of habit.

"What?" Gael asked.

I shrugged. "Nothing. I'm just glad we get to do this before college starts and we're both thrown into—"

"Sold out gigs and frat parties?" He raised a brow.

"No. Think more in the line of brooding over library books about coordinated vocal cords and lots of voice training until my throat's coarse."

"Sounds like fun." He pulled me behind him. "Come on."

In spite of my fear and insecurities at what lay before me, I couldn't wait to jump right in and put in the necessary work to become a star one day. It wasn't about the fame; all I wanted was to make my family proud and help my parents financially. They had battled poverty their whole life and deserved a break from it.

The customs officer asked something in Portuguese and Gael answered back for me. For a moment, the dark-haired woman regarded me intently, mouth pressed into a tight line, and then she nodded and motioned me to move along. I whispered a thank you and followed Gael to the hired limousine waiting for us.

As soon as we stepped out of the arrivals hall, a hot gust of air hit me in the face, making it hard to breathe until my lungs adjusted. I raised my hand to protect my eyes from the glaring brightness, and I'm not talking about the sun alone. There were so many people around us, dressed in all possible rainbow colors. I couldn't help but stare, hoping I didn't make a complete fool of myself—or worse, break a few country customs in the process. That's when a dark-haired guy caught my eyes.

He was tall, at least a few inches taller than the rest, with shaggy bed hair framing high cheekbones. His unbuttoned shirt revealed toned chest muscles and a dragon tattoo slithering south. My attention snapped from his cute face to his sculpted body you usually see in magazines. The guy was just hot. I rose on my toes to get a better look, but a redhead, about a head shorter than the guy, partly obstructed my view. Like on cue, both the guy and the girl turned to face me a moment before Gael opened the door to the limousine and I jumped on the backseat, losing sight of them.

"To the hotel?" the driver asked in broken English.

Gael nodded as I craned my neck, but the car sped off, leaving a trail of whirled up dust and torn newspaper pages in its wake. I sighed and sank into the plush leather seat, wondering what was wrong with me. My cheeks flushed with guilt. A wandering eye had never been my style. In fact, I prided myself on my loyalty toward my boyfriends. On the other hand, I hadn't really been looking that long. In fact, it was more of a glimpse from the corner of my eye. Sort of.

"You look flushed. Here, let me get you something to drink. I can't have you fainting on me now, can I?"

"I'm fine, thanks. Let's just get to the hotel." Maybe it was the heat that made me lethargic. I turned away, avoiding his probing gaze, guilt nagging at the back of my mind because he was a nice guy I really didn't deserve in that instant.

He reached over and grabbed a bottle of water together with what looked like a scarf "No. I insist. And I also insist on you wearing this."

I grabbed the bottle from his outstretched hand and took tiny sips because pleasing him was easier than arguing right now, then peered at the tiny scarf in his hands. The material was thin with the ending twisted to form a rope, and colored in dark brown and gold. I rubbed it between my fingers, marveling at how smooth and cold it felt.

"What is it?"

"A gift." He leaned in to tie it around my waist. "You can wear it as a belt."

I smiled. "Thanks. It's beautiful."

"It's a sad reality but tourists are kidnapped every day. I have connections down here. This scarf is given for protection. If you wear it, you'll be safe because people will know you belong to me and no one would dare touch you."

A belt to protect me from kidnappers? Sounded a bit ridiculous to me, but then again I knew almost nothing about this country. My smiled widened. "So I won't be abducted for ransom?"

"This is serious." His eyes hardened as he lifted my chin with his finger, forcing me to face him. His expression was dead serious. "Soph, I mean it. Don't take it off. Not even when you sleep."

27

I found his attitude strange, but I shrugged it off. I was used to him being strange every now and then. "Sure."

Gael pulled me against him and planted a kiss on my cheek, then started recalling his plans for the week. I tried hard to listen and nod at the right moments, but my mind kept wandering back to the guy with the tattoo. He had been stunning and yet I felt as though something else other than his looks drew me to him. Something that had been buried deep inside me for a long time. Like—something I couldn't quite pinpoint. Shaking my head slightly, I forced myself to tune into Gael's enthusiastic speech even though, for some unexplainable reason, I didn't feel in the slightest enthusiastic. Maybe all the sleepless nights got to me eventually because my brain wasn't making much sense. I was in Rio. I should be over the moon. And yet all I could suddenly think about was boarding the next plane home.

Half an hour later the limousine stopped in front of our hotel. To my surprise I found Gael hadn't booked a five-star hotel. With its big, ugly watermarks, hanging wires, scattered debris, and what reminded me of mildew in the crevices, this place had 'fell on hard times' written all over it. It didn't even look like a hotel, more like a neglected three-story building that hadn't seen a good scrub in the last ten years. I peered at the gaunt yellow grass that was supposed to be the front lawn and wondered why they didn't invest in a sprinkler system.

"Are we staying here?" I asked as the limousine driver pulled our suitcases out of the car and carried them into the lobby.

"Everything else was sold out," Gael said apologetically. "I forgot about the Brazilian Carnival. Do you mind?"

I wasn't aware the Brazilian Carnival took place at this time of the year, but I didn't comment. I shook my head. "No. Of course not. It's just that—" That what? That I had expected something much better? It wasn't like I lived in luxury. Was I slowly turning into a snob because I was dating a rich guy? Gael raised his brows so I continued, "You flew me first class, not to mention you picked me up in a fancy limousine. This took me by surprise, that's all. I never expected you to be comfortable in such a place."

"I guess you don't know everything about me," he said turning away so I didn't catch his expression.

"Actually, it's nice." Through squinted eyes it really didn't look that bad though I wouldn't have been surprised to find I had to share my bathroom with a few cockroaches.

Gael laughed and pulled me into the lobby. "At least we get to see a bit of the world famous Brazilian flair."

The hall was small but pretty with its walls covered in colorful carpeting with strange symbols. On the left, a dark-haired woman greeted us from behind a counter. I peered at the bellboy dressed in shorts and a flowery top as he disappeared up the stairs. A moment later, Gael and I followed behind, a set of keys dangling from Gael's fingers. The room, located on the first floor, had yet more flowery tapestry covering parts of the wall. The bright rays of sun seeping through the thin curtains cast an orange glow on the thick bedspread. Opposite from the four-poster bed was a dressing table and a TV set. The bed looked plain but nice enough to sleep. On the left, a door led into what I assumed was a walk-in cupboard. Above it, something strange caught my eye—three interlocking circles with a dot in its center. The entire rainbow-colored wall was adorned with all kinds of strange shapes and symbols, like something you might see on an Ouija board. I didn't know what to make of them. Obviously these people were into the occult or something. I wasn't exactly comfortable with it, but I figured everyone has the right to choose what religion they want to follow.

I pointed to a snake with red eyes painted on the left side of the wall murmuring, "I wonder what that means."

"In the voodoo culture, the serpent is a symbol of fertility," the bellboy said, grinning. "This place is magical. I bet you two will have plenty of babies together."

The thought almost made me choke on my breath. "That is if we ever get married. Not that I'm even anywhere near ready. I mean I want a career first and—"

"Gosh, don't even think about it. I'm not ready for babies either." Gael shook his head, laughing.

I let out a sigh of relief and pointed to a Celtic cross. "What does that one mean?"

"It's a crucifix within a circle," the bellboy went on to explain. "This ancient symbol is thought to protect one from spiritual dangers of all kinds. Anyone in this place is protected from demonic forces so they won't find you."

I smirked. "So I'm protected from demons and I'm going to have lots of babies. Gotta love this place."

"I don't believe in this kind of stuff for one minute," Gael whispered in my ear. "Do you?" I shook my head even though I actually did, but joking about it was way better than letting it freak me out.

Smiling, Gael tipped the bellboy and then locked the door as I looked at him, unsure how to put my concerns into words. In spite of dating him for a few months, we hadn't actually gotten as far as sleeping in the same bed. I knew he wasn't happy with it but I didn't care.

"I thought it'd be worse," Gael said, meaning the room.

"How so?" I asked.

"I didn't see mouse poop in the shower."

"Gross! I'm so glad I don't have to share my bed with those things." My laughter sounded fake even in my own ears.

He winked. "Yeah, it wouldn't be fair. They'd get to snuggle up to you while I was across the hall. The thought of you being all alone at night in a foreign county makes me nervous." His face suddenly became serious, lines hardening around his mouth.

"What? These people are nice. A little weird with their beliefs, but nonetheless sweet."

"You mustn't trust anyone. If someone tries to talk to you, don't say a word."

I nodded, not really taking him and his paranoia seriously. He didn't seem like he'd leave any time soon. I took a deep breath to steady my racing heart and decided to be upfront. "Are we both sleeping in here?"

"Only if you want to." A glint appeared in Gael's eyes. When I didn't react, he cleared his throat and pointed at the door. "There's an adjacent bedroom. We'll have to share the bathroom though." I breathed out relieved. I could definitely live with that.

"Sure. Just don't leave your clothes or bath towels all over the floor 'cause your maid isn't here to clean up after you. She's back in New York City."

"As long as you don't leave your blow dryer, make up, and lipsticks all over the sink and counter."

"You look beautiful today, even after a long flight," Gael said hoarsely. I smiled.

"I bet you're just are saying that so you get to sleep in here. Forget it, Mister." I punched his arm playfully. "You know I don't share my bed with anyone."

He tickled me. "Not even with me?"

Being the ticklish kind, I squealed and tried to push him away. "Not even with you. You know I need space."

"It really fits you." He touched my belt and leaned in to place a kiss on my lips. It wasn't unpleasant but I didn't quite enjoy it the way I should have. Slightly embarrassed at my own thoughts, I changed the topic.

"I wish you would've told me you had a gift."

"Don't worry about it. You do enough for me already." His eyes glittered and his thumb stroked my cheek. I knew it was an invitation of some kind but I didn't reply. For a moment, he regarded me as though he wanted to say something else, then turned around, calling over his shoulder, "Meet you for lunch in twenty."

Holding my breath, I waited until he disappeared through the door I had thought would lead into the closet. When I was finally alone, I took my time unpacking, stacking my clothes into the drawers and arranging my toiletries on top, then dropped on the bed to rest and gather my thoughts. A week alone with Gael, away from his busy schedule, our families and my money worries, and yet all I could think about was the tattooed guy at the airport and the moment our eyes connected. There had been something in his green gaze, something deep and twisted and unnatural.

I groaned at myself and closed my eyes, willing sleep to free my surprisingly vivid imagination from visualizing a guy I had seen for all of a few seconds.

"Soph." A hesitant voice broke through my bubble. Someone touched my arm gently. I opened my eyes groggily to stare at Gael's shape leaning over me. For a moment, I thought his eyes had turned black as coal, soaking up the light seeping in through the curtains. Whimpering, I pulled back from him. When I blinked, the vision was gone.

"Hey, it's just me," Gael whispered. "You had a bad dream."

I nodded and rubbed my head even though I couldn't remember having any dream. Just the pitch black I had been seeing for months now.

"Ready to get some food?" He held his hand out and I grabbed it, wondering how cold his skin felt in spite of the hot weather. He had changed into a pair of khaki slacks and a white shirt that made his tanned skin look darker.

"Yeah, great." I smiled and let him accompany me downstairs to the waiting limousine outside.

"You've been a bit strange lately," Gael started as soon as the driver sped off.

"How so?" My gaze met his. I hoped he couldn't see the turmoil inside me. Yes, I had been strange, but it wasn't because of anything he had done or said. I just didn't feel like myself. It was as if someone else dwelled inside my body, controlling my mind and emotions. I couldn't remember the last time I *hadn't* been jumpy and harried, just like my songs, but I guessed that's what the death of someone you were close to does to you. It makes you numb, dead inside.

Gael shrugged. "I don't know. Maybe distant?"

"I'm just tired, that's all." I leaned against his shoulder and wrapped my arm around his waist. He didn't react. "Sorry, I didn't notice. It's not you, it's me."

"Just don't let it affect us, okay?" I nodded in spite of my anger flaring up. I didn't like anyone telling me what to do, but he had a point. I couldn't let my personal problems destroy my friendship with Gael. I should've said 'relationship' but I knew that one had no future. For a second, I felt jealous at how well he handled his own personal loss of his brother.

Gael pulled me closer and planted a kiss on my forehead. "Good. Now let's focus on what we came for. I promised you a special time and that's exactly what you're getting."

"What did you have in mind?" I raised my brows at the secretive grin on his face.

"Just trust me."

The car stopped in front of a restaurant and we stepped out. A black shadow scooped over my head and perched on a nearby drainpipe. I raised my gaze against the glaring sun and peered at the large, black crow. The light caught in its beady eyes, making them shine like a black mirror for a moment. My heartbeat sped up even though I wasn't really surprised to see the bird. It couldn't be the same and yet I knew it was just as much as I had somehow known all along it'd be coming. Inclining my head lightly, I nodded at it, feeling instantly stupid. The bird let out a caw and flew away.

"I don't know about you but I'm starving," Gael said, pulling me through the open door.

"Yeah, me too." My stomach growled in agreement. We sat at the table near the window overlooking the busy street outside. As we ordered, the crow returned, perching down on the roof of the opposite building. Something told me it was there to watch. The uneasy feeling in the pit of my stomach returned as my appetite dissipated.

Chapter 3

Thrain

Under the hot Brazilian sun, I crouched down to the ground and touched the cracking earth, which wasn't so different to the one in Hell. Lucifer's instructions had been clear enough: find the girl, get her to obey Cassandra's command and save Dallas from sure death, and then get the hell out of there without any sort of involvement in the events that were about to unfold. And that's exactly what I planned to do because I had a career to think of and any sort of distraction wasn't an option.

Only a few days ago, Lucifer's daughter, Cassandra, had been a fallen angel: immortal and carefree though she had yet to turn eighteen and receive her full powers. After sneaking her mortal boyfriend, Dallas, into Hell and trying to trick him into marrying her to escape her curse, he was killed by an immortal vampire. Dallas's death sealed Cassandra's fate.

Having changed into a creature of the night now, half fallen angel half reaper, she sought pain and death to escape her own suffering.

With Dallas's physical death, she had changed. She had become more focused, more determined to reunite her lover's body with his wandering, lost soul, more demanding that I do as she said. Her wish was my command. As a demon of the highest order, I kept my promise to serve the dark princess. But I had to hurry up. She lived and breathed danger since she was only a few weeks away from turning into a full blooded reaper, a being that could rip one's throat to shreds with a flick of her claws. Obviously, I was more than eager to suck up to the future boss and not risk Lucifer's wrath by failing my mission and letting his only daughter turn into a creature roaming the threshold between life and death forever. So this mission mattered.

On the outskirts of Rio de Janeiro, I picked up Sofia's scent fairly quickly. It was the kind no tracker would miss, and certainly not someone like me. Cassandra stood a few steps away with her back leaned against the dirty wall of a newspaper kiosk, giving me space but still close enough to make the odd remark. I nodded to signal we were ready to leave. She inched closer but remained silent. The pain was written in the deep frown lines across her usually smooth forehead. Dark strands colored her otherwise red hair. I moistened my lips and looked away, feeling sorry for the agony she must be going through, for the emptiness she must feel at being separated from the man she loved.

"You don't need to do this," I whispered even though she could read my mind. "I'll find her and bring her to you."

She shook her head. "No, mate. This is my mission. I don't want you to do it for me."

"As you say, boss." I shrugged and turned away, squinting against the glaring sun as I focused on the multifaceted residues from Sofia's aura. She had been here not long ago. The trail stopped abruptly so she must've left in a car, but that didn't faze me. Now that I had her scent I would walk up and down this street until I found the direction she'd taken.

Half an hour later I was drenched in sweat and we were still searching.

"Do you have a cold?" Cass asked, smirking.

I shook my head. "That's not it. Something's wrong. I should've picked it up by now."

"Are you sure it's not just—" she waved her hand in the air, her long black nails that could morph into claws any second catching my attention "—that you're losing your touch?"

The softest hint of her earthy smell wafted past. Cass opened her mouth to speak again when I held up a finger to stop her, then pointed to our right. "This way."

"Looking to live forever? Because that is how long it's taking," she mumbled. I smiled and grabbed her hand, barely touching her ice-cold skin. It felt smooth like marble and thick as ice. She would turn soon, which I wouldn't wish upon my worst enemy, but at least I would get to be alone for a few hours without Lucifer's daughter watching over my shoulder. I couldn't quite focus with her around because her pain affected me. I didn't like my friends to suffer.

Maybe the solitude would help me do my job, because right now I was at my wit's end as to why I hadn't yet found Sofia.

Chapter 4

After a brief lunch, I was keen to return to the solitude of our hotel rooms to catch some sleep, but Gael seemed to have other plans.

"Where are we going?" I asked for the umpteenth time.

"You'll see." His eyes twinkled mischievously. I smiled pretending to be excited, commenting on the beauty of the town we were in. Truth was, I didn't feel excited in the least. I actually feared secrets because they made me feel like I was opening Pandora's box. I appreciated Gael's efforts and I knew he meant well, but as much as I tried, I felt so disconnected from him. Ever since the airport, my mind seemed preoccupied and distanced.

The vehicle raced through the busy streets, past crowds of people gathering in front of dilapidated taverns. Eventually, the vehicle took another right turn onto unpaved terrain, leaving the city behind.

Looking out of the window, I saw people, dressed in barely more than rags, their faces worn out and tired. The houses we passed by were huts made of what looked like cardboard boxes. In front of them, children played and laughed the way only children can. My throat tightened as I watched all these people struggling with poverty, mothers holding their babies in their arms in sanitary conditions not fit for a newborn, children with no future. I felt a sense of hopelessness creep over me. The children reminded me of my own childhood far away from the luxury of Western civilization. Life had been hard for my family, but we made the most of it. We appreciated the simple things: our family, our friends and that we had so much to be thankful for, such as our lives. I remembered how we used to snuggle together under a thin sheet when the Russian winter enveloped the vast lands in a white blanket that could freeze a grown man to death within a few hours. And every spring we were grateful to have survived.

The driver stopped to ask for directions and motioned a kid to come closer. The child obeyed and inched closer, unaware of the danger that might be lurking in a stranger's vehicle. At the boy's sight, barely older than ten with dark curls and torn shorts, something broke inside. I wiped a tear from the corners of my eyes, hoping Gael wouldn't notice, and reached into my purse for money.

"What are you doing?" Gael hissed.

I ignored him as I rolled down the window and handed the kid a few banknotes, watching his eyes widen for a moment before his hand clasped around the money. He said something, which I interpreted as thank you.

Gael grabbed my arm tightly that it hurt a little, forcing me to face him. "What's wrong with you? Don't do that ever again. You can't just walk in here and advertise how rich you are, unless you don't mind a bullet through your head."

I pulled my arm away, irritated, anger rising inside me. He was right, of course, and yet deep in my heart I couldn't care less. Gael knew nothing about poverty, but I had experienced it first hand. The car sped off again.

"Look, I'm sorry," Gael whispered into my ear. It's all about your safety. I couldn't live with myself if something happened to you."

"I'm old enough to know what I should or shouldn't do."

He nodded and a glint appeared again in his eyes, flickering like a candle flame and disappearing a second later. We drove in silence for another five minutes up what looked like a tiny hill with wilted grass and garbage to either side. The car stopped again, this time in front of a hut larger than the ones we had passed. Even though there were other houses around, the area looked less crowded with larger front yards and fences barely reaching my knees. A stray chicken jumped on top of the front car hood, not minding us as we got out. I could hear pigs squealing and a horse neighing, and figured this must be some sort of ranch.

My sandals sank into a hard layer of dirt as I looked around. In spite of all the dust and the garbage lining the street, the yard looked clean with a stony path leading to a cottage with whitewashed walls and dried herbs hanging from the windowsills. Colorful ribbons hanging from the branches of a thin tree swayed with a soft breeze. Gael grabbed my hand and pulled me behind him as he whispered, "Come on."

I followed even though uneasiness settled in the pit of my stomach, making me gasp for air. As we took slow steps down the path, sweat gathered on my forehead and poured down my back. I raised my hand to wipe my brows when I noticed a crow circling the sky and perching down on one of the branches. Slowly, the crow was starting to creep me out, not least because I knew it was the same one as before. But how could a crow follow me from New York to Rio? It didn't make any sense. I stopped in mid-stride and peered up at its magnificent black wings and beady eyes. The animal's beak opened as though to speak to me.

"We don't have time for admiring the wildlife," Gael said, pulling my arm. I nodded and let him drag me away and through the door into the hut.

From inside, the room seemed quite spacious with fur covering the bare ground. The air smelled of dried herbs and incense. To the right was a stone lined hearth with a large cooking pan and a mattress set up in front of it. To the left, an old woman, clad in a white summer dress reaching down to her ankles and with tan skin, sat at a kitchen table, bowed over a large bucket, cutting string beans. She stood as she saw us and wiped her hands on her dress, her skinny body moving with surprising agility and grace. Her eyes, framed by countless wrinkles, met mine and for a moment I forgot to breathe. Her green gaze bore into mine, reaching deep inside my soul like claws. I stumbled a step backward, fighting the invading sensation of something searching through the layers of my emotions laying bare the secrets I had been trying to hide from both myself and those around me for years.

"Madame Estevaz," Gael said, reaching out his hand. She ignored it as she continued to stare at me. The feeling of uneasiness inside my stomach intensified.

"This is the girl?" she asked in broken English.

"Yes," Gael said.

"Hm." She drew closer and placed a hand on my forehead, then pointed to the mattress. I glanced at Gael. When he nodded reassuringly, I followed Madame Estevaz to the hearth. After some resistance, I gave in to Gael's persistent request and laid down on the mattress.

"Wait outside," Madame Estevaz said to Gael.

He shook his head. "I need to be present. Surely you understand."

The old woman's mouth pressed into a tight line, but she kept quiet as she grabbed a brown pot with what looked like dried bones and started spreading them around me. I eyed them, disgusted, making sure I wouldn't touch them.

"What's this about?" I asked. What did Gael have in mind? I trusted him, but the whole situation was too macabre for my taste. In my head, I recalled all the reasons why I hated surprises.

"She's about to find out your future," Gael said.

I raised my chin defiantly, ready to jump up and make a run for the nearest exit. "I don't want anyone to tell me my future."

"We came all the way for this. I thought you'd appreciate it," Gael said. The glint from before returned, and for a brief second I thought I saw something dark in his eyes, just like that afternoon when he startled me out of my sleep. My temper flared. I shook my head, wondering what was wrong with me. First the hallucinations, now my inability to control myself. I lay down on the mattress and nodded at Madame Estevaz, ignoring the nagging voice at the back of my mind.

"Close your eyes and relax. Don't fight it," Gael said softly.

My heart started to hammer against my ribcage as I closed my eyes, letting the darkness, which had been beckoning to me for a while, engulf me. Madame

Estevaz called out in her native tongue. A second later, loud drumming echoed through the air, startling me. I opened my eyes when something soft covered my face. It was a black scarf that barely filtered the daylight. I was glad to find I see through the thin material.

Madame Estevaz began to hum next to me, a soft murmur growing louder that seemed to accompany the tiny drum in her hand. Her words were coming sharp, hurting my ears even though I had no idea what they meant. The mattress began to shift to the left and right like a boat floating on water. Something moved across my skin; cold iron fingers grabbed hold of my arms and clasped tightly. I felt fear rise inside me. This didn't feel right. I scanned the air frantically but there was nothing there to touch me.

Gael. My mouth opened but no sound found its way out of my throat. I peered down at my naked arms where the skin looked pushed in as though invisible fingers were pressing down on my limbs. Coldness climbed up my chest and built a shield around my heart.

And then the pain began, cutting through me like an arrow Long pangs of it that made breathing impossible. The voice in my head screamed louder than Madame Estevaz's incantations. Another rush of pain cut through me, and my body went into spasms. I felt my eyes roll in their sockets. Something emerged beside me and I knew instantly it was no mortal and nothing I had ever seen. *Please.* My mind was barely able to form the words, imploring the creature to go away and leave me alone, but I knew if it could hear me it wouldn't listen. The cold sensation around my heart grew stronger, reminding me of thousands of ice picks piercing my skin. I was so cold and yet my body was burning. A thin sheen of sweat covered me, soaking my skimpy clothes. My head moved to the side frantically as panic rose inside me. I had never been so scared in my life.

Outside, the crow cawed, warning me. When the pain hit again, I clenched my teeth, ready to wait it out. But this time it didn't stop. For a long time, all I could feel were coldness and piercing pain that wouldn't ebb.

Chapter 5

Thrain

After Cass disappeared, I spent hours looking around Rio. For some inexplicable reason, my abilities wouldn't pick up Sofia's trail, even though I couldn't think of anything else. Ever since catching a glimpse of her at the airport, her face kept popping up in my mind, making focusing on anything else impossible. I attributed it to the immense pressure on me. Not only would I lose my rank and would never be able to return to my Origin. If I failed, I had no idea what Lucifer would do to me, and I certainly had no intention to find out.

The hospital was a large building with paint peeling from the yellow walls. There were a total of five stories with the emergency department situated on the ground floor. As I walked in, I knew exactly where I'd find Cass.

"Olá. Posso ajudá- lo?" the receptionist, a dark-haired woman in her late thirties, asked with a smile.

Even though I understand her Portuguese perfectly well, I shook my head and muttered in a fake French accent, "Não falo português." I shot her an apologetic smile and walked past, knowing all too well she wouldn't follow me and make a fuss. It would be too much of a hassle arguing with a large guy like me. In a few long strides, I reached the double doors leading to the emergency department and walked into what I assumed was the busiest area of the building.

Drama and suffering was palpable in the air. Doctors and nurses in blood stained uniforms hurried up and down the narrow corridor, paying me no attention. I strolled down the hall, hoping to blend in so I wouldn't need to use my shape shifting abilities. A young nurse shot me an interested look, but she didn't stop me as I walked past.

I followed Cass's trail—a thin thread of black fog that characterized all reapers—to one of the ER rooms where two patients lay on white beds, hooked up to various whirring machines that wouldn't be able to keep them alive for much longer. I knew where to find Cass, because a reaper like her would never hover around a person that was more dead than alive.

She stood near one of the beds, back pressed against the white wall, her still emerald green eyes shining unnaturally as they soaked up the pain wafting past. In this stadium, Cass had long

50

transferred into the world in-between and no mortal could see her. But some could feel her presence.

"Cass?" I touched her shoulder. She barely raised her gaze from one of the two humans. For a moment, I saw her shoulders slump in defeat, her expression haunted by grief and sadness, and then her ecstasy returned. Soaking up the pain of others relieved her own, only to come back full force within a few hours, turning her more and more into this thing that couldn't stay away from death. I shuddered. Having known Cass for a long time, I knew she never wanted any of this. I felt pity for her.

"Cass, I know you can hear me." I shook her arm lightly. Her skin, black as coal, felt colder than before and her green gaze darkened. In this in-between state of the physical and spiritual realm, where her body morphed into a reaper, her skin couldn't warm up as long as she wasn't dead. She raised her chin a notch, black eyes glinting unnaturally. Her lips peeled back, revealing a string of white teeth. I didn't know whether she was laughing or in pain, but it sure creeped me out.

The left patient on the bed stirred in his sleep, drawing his breath several times before his heart stopped beating and the little ECG machine next to him started beeping. Cass sucked in her breath, relishing the moment when the man's life force waned. She inched closer and pushed her hands inside his ribcage. Only then did I notice the razor sharp claws she had been hiding behind her back that

51

now tore through the man's astral body as he rose to hover over his body.

"Time to go." Cass's voice was surprisingly calm and composed given the ecstasy she must be feeling. With a snap of her fingers she snapped the silver thread that held the man's astral body attached to his physical carcass. And then she disappeared with him, leaving me behind to look at the whirring machines and the deceased who had just passed away in his sleep. I sighed and walked out of the building, then sat down on a nearby bench as I prepared for the half hour wait. Cass would be back soon with a refreshed mind that would be free of the usual pain for a few hours. I grabbed a newspaper and let my mind switch off for a while, but my thoughts kept circling back to the girl with the dyed jet-black hair. For some reason, I couldn't shake off the way she had looked at me, curious yet cool and composed. She was a mortal, I wasn't, so getting up close and personal with her wasn't an option.

***

Half an hour later, Cass appeared behind me, her cheeks a glowing pink, eyes shining emerald green again with renewed vigor and life force. I folded the newspaper and tossed it aside as I made room for her to sit next to me, but she just shook her head, preferring to stand.

JAYDE SCOTT

"How is he?" I asked, meaning her mate, Dallas.

"Still dead." She shrugged as though it didn't matter. It was her way to deal with her emotions. I nodded sympathetically as she asked, "Did you find Sofia's trail yet?"

I shook my head. "Nope, but I found something else." She sat down, her flowing dress grazing my arm as she leaned in, interested. "One of your vampire friends is around. I caught his scent."

"Who?"

"The car racer."

"Kieran?" she asked, raising her brows. I nodded. "What's he doing here?" From her expression and her sharp tone, I could tell she wasn't happy.

"No idea." I lowered my voice. "Maybe he's trying to help."

"Or mess things up. They wanted to come." She peered to the car park on the other side of the road, and I knew instantly any chance of doing this my way was slowly dissipating into thin air.

"Who?" I asked even though I could smell them now. Dallas's sister, Amber, and her vampire boyfriend, Aidan, stood waiting somewhere in the distance, out of view.

"You're good but you should've smelled them much earlier. What's wrong with you? Do you have a blocked nose?"

53

I had been wondering about the same thing, minus the blocked nose. As an immortal, I didn't experience the usual health problems. Ignoring her question, I got up and waved, knowing the vampires were watching me. "A big family reunion then," I muttered under my breath.

"Trust me, I'm about as excited as you are, but Amber wouldn't let me leave without her. And where Amber is, Aidan will follow," Cass whispered. "This family reunion blows."

"Let's face the dragon then." I grabbed Cass's arm and pulled her after me.

They were waiting in the shadows even though their skin wouldn't burn from the sun. Aidan was a foot taller than Amber, but I noticed her first. She had only recently been turned into a vampire, but her skin already showed that unnatural paleness.

Even though Aidan was a foot taller than her, I noticed Amber first. I could see the glint in her eyes from a few feet. She had only recently been turned into a vampire, but her skin already showed an unnatural paleness, which she tried to cover with a black long sleeved top and jeans that only made her skin look paler, white as snow. Aidan didn't fare any better, and his unnaturally blue eyes didn't help his cause.

"You're blending right in, dude." I held out my hand, grinning. Aidan reached out but Amber grabbed it first, her hazel gaze meeting mine. She squeezed tight.

"Thrain, right?"

I nodded. "We met before when you were the damsel in distress. Seems like things have changed."

A smile lit up her face. "You could say that. I went from alive to dead to alive again."

I smirked. "You have a broad definition of alive then."

"We should get going," Aidan said, grabbing her elbow as though to protect her. The chick certainly didn't need protection, but she kept silent. "Meet us at the hotel?" Without waiting for my answer, they dissipated into thin air.

"Still the same control freak, I see," I muttered to Cass as we neared our car, hating the fact that, between portals, we had to travel like mortals in the physical realm while the vampires got to teleport to places without being stuck in traffic. I didn't like that they had this advantage over the inhabitants of Hell. Cass had a phone that could open a portal anywhere, but with all the potential witnesses around us it was safer to just drive.

"He'll get the job done," Cass said.

I peered at the tight lines around her mouth, wondering what she was hiding. "What job? I thought it was mine."

She nodded as she opened the car door and slumped down into the passenger seat. "It is. But you're a tracker and he's the bounty hunter."

"What do you need a bounty hunter for?"

"You said Kieran's around." She turned to face me as I started the engine, letting the car idle on the spot. "Kieran's a bounty hunter too. Aidan doesn't know his brother's here, which means he's looking for something." I raised my brows, still not getting where this was heading. Cass groaned and pointed at my forehead. "Yo, could you turn that thing up there on? Kieran was the one who turned Amber and the Lore court knows it, meaning until now he's been hiding. Why would he leave his hiding place, unless he made a deal with someone?"

I nodded, even though I still had no idea what she was talking about. "What's he doing here from all the places in the world?"

"Right. Okay, let's go." She slumped into her seat. I didn't move.

"You knew Kieran was here." She didn't answer, which I took as a confirmation. Dammit, something was wrong with me, or why would she pick up a vampire's scent long before me? "Just say it."

She shook her head. "Wouldn't be good for your ego, mate."

I set my jaw. "When?"

"At the airport. That's why I went to pick up Amber and Aidan. If Kieran's looking for something, we need to find it first. And who's better at picking clues than a bounty hunter?"

"I'm a tracker."

She rolled her eyes. "Yeah, I know that. But right now you can't even find Sofia. With me

56

incapacitated because of this horrible curse and your blocked nose—" she waved her hand in my face "—let's just say, we might not be able to find Sofia, get her to do the job and keep an eye on Kieran if we stumble upon him. Besides, they're brothers, so the chance they'll screw each other over is very unlikely."

And then I understood what she was saying. In the paranormal world, everyone was your enemy. What were the odds of someone employing Kieran to be in the same place at the same time as us? Whoever employed Kieran could only have harm in mind, and the moron probably didn't even know it.

"Have you told Aidan?"

"And miss all the drama?" She snorted. "Are you kidding me?" I could smell the excitement wafting from her, passing on to me. Grinning, I dodged the oncoming traffic as I changed lanes. My foot hit the accelerator hard. Time to let the chaos demon in me out and get this job done.

Chapter 6

For a long time all I could hear was yelling in a language I didn't understand. The words sounded accusatory and angry, but I wasn't sure whether they were aimed at me, or someone else. The entity was gone, but I felt cold, colder than I had ever been in my entire life, the freezing sensation competing with the pain in my chest. But that wasn't what worried me in my dream-like state. That scary darkness from my dreams was all around me, enveloping me and keeping me hostage in my own body and mind. No matter how hard I tried to push and pry my eyes open, I couldn't move. Slowly, I started to panic, wondering whether I'd ever wake up and be my old self again.

I felt trapped, I felt bodiless. I felt panic rising inside me whether I'd ever wake up. I thought of my family, of what would happen to them if they heard I was gone. Gone, how final those words sounded. As if I was dead already. Was I dead?

I didn't know how long I lingered in that empty yet painful state, drifting in and out of consciousness. When my eyes finally fluttered open, I realized I was in my hotel room, propped up on a pillow in the middle of my bed. The clock on my nightstand showed it was already after 10 p.m. Gael sat beside me. When I stirred, he smiled and grabbed my hand. Something flickered in his eyes. It was the same dark shadow I had seen before, like a black flame lapping at dried wood, only this time my mind was fully operational and I knew I wasn't imagining things. I pulled back from him, but only a little.

"Hey, it's me," Gael said. "You were out of it for a while."

I swallowed and moistened my dry lips. "What happened?" My voice came low and hoarse, as though I hadn't spoken in days.

He held a glass of water to my lips and I took greedy gulps. The cool liquid soothed the scratchy sensation at the back of my throat. "You passed out from the heat."

I shook my head. "Something else must've happened. I remember the fortune teller starting her chatter, and then there was blackness." I shivered as I let my memories invade my mind. That was one scary place I never wanted to visit again.

"Trust me, it was the heat." Gael set his jaw, signaling the conversation was over. The black flame in his eyes flickered again. I finished my water and put the glass back on the bedside table.

"What did the fortune teller say?" I asked.

"What?"

I turned to face him. "She spoke for hours. I want to know what she said."

"Don't be ridiculous. When you passed out, we wrapped you in damp towels and I drove you home. You've been sleeping since the early afternoon." I peered at him. Somehow I knew he was lying, which didn't make sense. Why would he avoid telling the truth? Unless the woman had said something bad and he didn't want to upset me. I grabbed his hand and gave it a light squeeze, wondering why his skin felt cold as ice in spite of the smoldering heat outside.

"What did she say?" I persisted.

Ignoring my question, Gael got up and headed for the door, calling over his shoulder, "Why don't you take a shower while I get us dinner? I won't be long, and don't take off the scarf."

I stared after him, perplexed. Something wasn't right. I could tell from the way he treated me. He had never been this brisk before. Gael wasn't the most open and talkative person, but he had never been this secretive, brushing me off for no apparent reason. Did I say or do anything wrong?

Eventually I got up and stripped off my clothes, leaving the scarf wrapped around my wrist, then jumped under the shower. I slumped against the cold tiles, letting the hot water trickling down every part of my aching body before I went about checking my arms for any bruises where I thought fingers had pressed into my skin. There were none.

I turned off the water tap and stepped out, wrapping a large towel around me. The mirror had misted over with steam. I swiped my hand across its smooth surface and regarded myself. My large blues eyes were hooded, as though I hadn't slept in ages. My hair hung in thick wet strands. And then, for a split second, I heard something: a scratching noise, like nails on a chalkboard, but so low I wasn't sure it had been there at all. I checked the door, which was closed, then went back to the mirror, figuring I was imagining things again. When I picked up my brush to comb my hair, I could see in the reflection of the mirror that the window had misted over as though someone had breathed on it from the outside. A tiny drawing appeared. I turned my head sharply, noticing small lines on the glass. Frowning, I inched closer to read the word: PLEH. Someone staying here before me must've been dissatisfied with his vacation and written it. I couldn't agree more. Ignoring it, I turned back to the mirror to pull my hair into a messy ponytail, when the writing caught my eye again. In the mirror, PLEH spelt backwards: HELP.

My breathing accelerated, my heart racing in my chest a million miles an hour. The room was situated on the second floor with no balcony and no back garden. Someone must be playing a prank on me. Even though the voice at the back of my mind screamed to stay away, I removed the hatch and pushed the window wide open, leaning over the sill as much as I could. The space below was so tiny, one couldn't hide a flowerpot let alone an adult. Besides, a stonewall reached from the ground almost as high as the first floor. Unless someone had a pair of wings and could fly over it, I doubted they could climb over, breathe against the window and then dissipate into thin air a moment later.

I closed the window again. The writing was still there and for the first time I noticed the lines looking messy, like those of a child. The letter P ended with a tiny swirl. My sister, Theo, used to do that. Something clicked into place inside me. I had a strong feeling that it all made sense and yet I couldn't explain it. A cawing echoed outside. A moment later, a black crow perched on the windowsill, its beady gaze meeting mine. For the first time I was relieved to see her so I nodded and I swear she nodded back. Behind me the door burst open, startling me. I turned to see Gael enter.

"Ever heard of knocking?" I snapped.

"I knocked, but you didn't reply." He raised an eyebrow as he peered from me to the window and then back at me. "What are you doing?"

I followed his line of vision to see the crow was gone. "Taking a shower, like you said. Hope you brought dinner 'cause I'm starving." I walked past him, ignoring the hesitation on his face. I knew I should tell him everything, but something held me back. If he kept secrets from me then so would I. Besides, how could I explain what just happened without sounding like a lunatic who belonged into the nearest loony bin.

"I did," Gael said.

"Let me change first." Without waiting for an answer, I slammed the door behind me and grabbed clean clothes from the wardrobe, then slipped into my underwear, a pair of jeans and a baggy top, wrapping Gael's scarf around my waist because I figured just doing what he had instructed would save me a possible confrontation.

On the bedspread were disposable plates and cutlery next to a brown bag I assumed contained our dinner. The strong aroma of fried chicken hung heavy in the air. I slumped down next to them and piled food onto the plates as Gael joined me. I could tell he was still preoccupied from the deep frown across his forehead and the vacant expression.

"Not hungry?" I pointed at the untouched chicken wings in front of him. He managed a half-smile and took a bite. "Care to elaborate why you wouldn't tell me what really happened at the fortune teller's place?"

He let out an exaggerated sigh and turned to face me. A strange glint played in his eyes. So I wasn't imagining things. I bit down on my lip but didn't comment. "I told you nothing happened, Sofia. Why won't you just drop it? You're being ridiculous."

I nodded and met his gaze as he stared at me, cold and calculating. He was lying. Only then did I notice, after being out of it for an entire afternoon, he didn't even ask how I was. I had seen it before. My father had been that way. Not from early on, but after he had fallen out of love with my mother. But maybe he had never been in love with her. I moistened my lips and turned away.

"What's wrong?" Gael asked as though sensing my emotional undercurrents. I shook my head and smiled, wondering what I was doing here. I had never been in love with him. To expect something I couldn't give was just wrong. He had been my rock when Sofia died. Gratitude was about all I felt for him right now. For some inexplicable reason, I actually felt bad for it.

"Thanks for dinner," I said.

"Sure. I have some business to attend to. Why don't you get some rest and I'll see you in the morning?"

"Sounds good." I raised my cheek to him, more out of habit than of true need. He planted a sloppy kiss on my forehead, probably feeling just as disconnected as I did.

"Stay inside," Gael said. His tone was nonchalant, but the order didn't fail to register. I watched him walk across the tiny room and close the door behind him without so much as a good night. Maybe the guy had something on his mind, or he was indeed busy, but something didn't quite add up and I was eager to solve the mystery.

Deep in thought, I stacked the remnants of our dinner inside its packaging, considering whether to throw it all into the waste bin. I had never been a fan of smelly rooms so I waited a few more minutes to make sure Gael wouldn't come back, then slipped my naked feet into my trainers and opened the door.

The hall was empty, devoid of any signs of someone's presence. I closed the door behind me and tiptoed down the oriental carpet to the staircase all the while holding my breath as I listened for any sound. My heart hammered in my chest even though it was ridiculous since I had nothing to hide. Gael had instructed me to stay inside, but I was a grown up and no one had the right to tell me what to do. If he caught me and disapproved, he could just shove it where the sun don't shine.

For a moment, I hesitated in the doorway. When nothing stirred, I walked down the stairs to the ground floor. The entrance hall was just as deserted, so no one there to ask. Figuring the garbage bins had to be outside, I took the backdoor that led into a tiny communal garden. The moon was partly behind by thick clouds but gave enough light to see clear shapes. I scanned the area as my eyes adjusted. To my right, large bushes obstructed my view of what was behind. To my left, a large wall protected the hotel from the outside world. I saw nothing that resembled garbage bins but I wasn't ready to give up yet, not least because I enjoyed the cool air and the solitude.

The soft breeze left a cool sensation on my skin, turning it into goosebumps. I breathed in the crisp air and walked down the tiny path toward the bushes, then stopped in my tracks when I heard male voices. They were too low to understand, so I crept closer until I could make out one of them was Gael. I crouched next to one of the bushes and squeezed my hand through to part the leaves so I could catch a glimpse of what was happening on the other side.

I recognized Gael immediately by the light brown slacks and the white shirt he had worn half an hour ago when he brought up dinner. He had his back turned toward me. As he talked, his voice betrayed irritation. The other guy was a few inches taller than Gael with dark hair that brushed the black collar of his shirt. He was clad in blue jeans that showed off strong legs, but what caught my attention immediately were his striking blue eyes. I had never seen blue eyes like that, shining in the dark without any light source reflecting in them. My gaze moved to the pale skin of his face and neck. I, too, liked to shy the sun, but he was at least a shade paler and it made him look unnatural, not in a sick way but different.

"How many times do I need to tell you I don't have much time?" Gael's voice cut through the silence of the night.

"I heard you the first time," the blue-eyed guy said.

"Obviously, you didn't otherwise you would have found what I'm looking for."

"There's been a complication."

"Really?" Gael snorted. "And why would I care? You're being paid to do your job. How you do it is your business. As long as I pay all I want to hear about or see is results."

I scoffed inwardly, wondering why Gael was being such a jerk. That was no way to talk to a dog, let alone a human being. As though reading my thoughts, the blue-eyed guy's gaze shifted toward me and for a moment my breath caught in my throat. His sudden smile seemed out of place for someone who was being lectured by his boss, and yet I knew it wasn't addressed at Gael. It was for me. He knew I was there, hiding in the shadows.

I straightened my back, ready to dash for the house before the blue eyed guy betrayed my presence, but Gael beat me to it.

"You have twenty-four hours to get the job done. Better not waste my time," Gael called over his shoulder as he stomped past, unaware of my presence, his arrogance mirroring in his stride. Holding my breath, I waited until I heard the backdoor open and close behind him. Only then did I dare to turn around and my heart jumped in my throat.

He was standing right next to me, peering down with the same unnerving smile.

"Looking for something?" His voice was deep and low, barely more than a whisper. "I'm Kieran."

He reached out his hand and I grabbed it, for some inexplicable reason trusting him.

"Sofia," I said, pointing at the bag in my hand. "I was throwing out the garbage."

"That's not the only thing you should be throwing out." Even in the darkness, I could see the twinkle in his eyes.

Ignoring his remark, I moistened my lips. "What was that all about? What's Gael looking for?" I knew it was none of my business, and yet I couldn't keep my curiosity at bay. His loyalty or work ethic would keep him from answering anyway, or so I thought.

"He's looking for a blade," Kieran said.

"You mean like a knife?" I stared at him dumbfounded.

Kieran shrugged. "Sort of an oversized one. Let's just say it could do more than prick your finger."

He couldn't be serious. Yet, his expression remained earnest. No flicker of a smile that he was joking. What would Gael need a blade for, unless it was a collector's item and worth a lot? I didn't ask because in my head I already had my explanation.

"Have I answered all your questions, Sofia?" The way he spoke my name almost made me giggle. His gaze regarded me up and down and then up again, settling somewhere below my chin. The telltale heat of a blush crossed my cheeks.

"You have. Thank you," I said, my voice surprisingly calm.

"Good. Then I hope you'll take my word of advice and go away from here as fast as you can. Far, far away. This is no place for a girl like you." He leaned in and planted a soft kiss on my cheek, then turned on his heel and...disappeared. Literally. I stared at the empty space where he had just stood a few seconds ago. My pulse gained in speed. Was something wrong with my head and I had just imagined things? First the man in the club, and now this one here. No one just dissolved into nothing. That was the stuff of action hero movies. It didn't happen in real life because it wasn't possible, not real. And yet I knew I had seen him and he had talked to me. Maybe he had a trick up his sleeve, like being pulled up in the air by invisible cords.

The breeze whipped my hair against my cheeks, jolting me out of my thoughts. Even though I didn't want to, I returned to the safety of my room, still holding the bag with the rest of our dinner in my hands. Kieran's words rang through my mind over and over again. He had advised that I leave, but my vacation had just started. I wondered what he had meant by 'no place for a girl like you'. Was this part of Rio dangerous? That certainly made sense. But I figured Gael wouldn't risk our lives if he knew the place wasn't ideal for tourists.

I entered my room and let out a shriek when I noticed the figure sitting on my bed. It took my brain a second to realize it was Gael. His face was contorted with rage, his brows were drawn together.

"I told you to stay inside." His voice dripped with accusation.

"Had to take out the garbage." I shrugged, forcing myself not to roll my eyes.

"The garbage bins are behind the house." His gaze fell on the bag in my hands, and he cocked a brow.

"That explains why I didn't find them."

"When I say I want you to stay inside, that's exactly what I mean. You have no excuse for venturing out," Gael said.

I turned to face him, my eyes throwing daggers. "I don't appreciate the way you're talking to me. In case you haven't noticed, I'm not your child."

"I know that," Gael said, slowly. "But you have to understand I was worried about you. You're in a different country. I've been here before. Brazil can be dangerous, so it's for your own safety."

"Fair enough." I felt myself soften. He had a point. It wasn't his fault he couldn't express his concern in a less controlling way. I smiled and slumped down on the bed, regretting it instantly. I could only hope he wasn't taking it as an invitation. He didn't.

"Just stay inside," Gael said before leaving.

I stared after him, seriously struggling to make sense of his attitude. One part of me tried hard to defend him while the other knew there was no excuse for it. Whether I liked it or not, he was being a jerk. I had seen it before, the tiny signs that indicated a controlling personality, but I figured having a boyfriend was better than being alone, particularly when I still missed my sister. Maybe it was time to call in a break until I knew whether this relationship was indeed what I wanted.

Leaning against the pillows, I untied the shawl from around my waist and tossed it on the floor. When guilt nagged at me, I got up and stacked it inside one of the drawers. The noise of flapping wings started almost instantly. A few weeks ago, I would've turned the room upside down to find out where it came from, but now I just snuggled under the blanket and pressed the pillows against my ears to drown out the unnerving noise. It was past midnight when I finally managed to fall asleep with Kieran's mysterious eyes and warning still lingering at the periphery of my mind.

Chapter 7

Thrain

When Cass and I arrived at the hotel, Amber and Aidan were already waiting. I could sense the tension between them. Ever since Amber had been turned into a vampire, she kept blaming it on him, which didn't surprise me. Most mortals glamourized our world and actively searched for us, but not Amber. Maybe because she had almost died at the hands of Aidan when he sucked her dry. As if that weren't enough, her brother, Dallas, had died after the Shadows helped a blood-crazed vampire, who happened to be Aidan's ex, break into Hell to retrieve the famous book of the Shadows. Cass had stolen it from the Shadows only a few weeks previously. Seeing it from this perspective, it was all her fault, which she kept saying over and over again. Several times I tried to tell her that it was fate and Dallas's death would've happened anyway, but she couldn't be consoled. And so I just gave up and listened instead, keeping my thoughts to myself.

Our hotel accommodation was a whole penthouse suite, courtesy of Cass's father. Groaning, I dropped down on the couch in our living room, wishing I could just do this myself. A bunch of people would just slow me down. As if on cue, Aidan started taking over.

"I say we split up to comb through the city. Amber and I start on one side, and Cass and you on the other."

I snorted. "You call *that* a plan? It makes no sense. For one, we're immortals. Why would we have to split into two groups when we could all work alone and be twice as fast? And second, I can pick up her scent in an instant."

"Why haven't you already then?" Amber raised her thin brows. "You need us, whether you want it or not."

"She's right," Cass said from her seat at the window.

"Which part?" I mumbled. That I still hadn't picked up her scent, or that I needed them to get this mission done. I pressed my lips shut and bit the inside of my cheek to keep back a remark. I had never failed to find someone. In fact, I had been the one to find and break into Shadow land, something no one else had ever done before me. If I could find my way through magic, then I surely could pick up the scent of a mortal. I snorted as I slumped deeper into my seat, rubbing my temple in desperate need of a plan.

"Okay, so the shape shifter's in charge here now?" Amber said, pointing at me. "'Cause if he is, he's just wasting time sitting on his backside while my brother's life is hanging by a thread."

"Technically, he's already dead," I mumbled. Cass shot me a venomous look. I shrugged. "What? It's true."

Well, thanks for telling her, moron. Cass's voice echoed in my mind.

Amber pushed Aidan back, sending him tumbling against the wall. As a new vampire, she obviously still couldn't control her powers, which would keep coming and going for a few years. "You said he's still alive." She poked a finger into Cass's chest.

"He is, somewhere on one of Heaven's dimensions," Cass said.

Amber's eyes were ablaze with fury. "It's all your fault. If you didn't abduct him to Hell, he'd still live. I'll never forgive you."

"It wasn't her fault," Aidan said, pulling Amber back. For a long moment, she just stared at him, locked in that battle they seemed to keep having. I had no idea how the guy could live with her constant blame. Praise the Fates my mate wasn't mortal. Though I had yet to meet her.

Eventually Amber retreated to the back of the room, but her shoulders remained tense, her chin raised defiantly. Aidan breathed out, relieved, and joined her, wrapping his arm around her shoulders to draw her close. I could feel the comforting waves wafting from him as he tried to influence her emotions to calm her down.

I sucked in a deep breath to gather my thoughts before I spoke. "I'm outta here."

"Where are you going?" Cass asked.

"Doing my job. And don't ask if you can come 'cause the answer's no. I'm better off on my own." I slammed the door shut, not waiting for an answer. Like her father, Cass could be quite persuasive, so I'd rather not give her a chance to demonstrate her authoritarian nature.

The afternoon sun shined down relentlessly as I took the backdoor and jumped over the fence onto the beach promenade. The Big Boss hadn't skimped on hotel costs when he chose this location. Maybe he had hoped his only daughter would enjoy her last two weeks on earth before she'd turn into a reaper...unless I found Sofia. As I walked down the promenade to the beach, my shoes leaving a trail in the soft sand, I smiled at some girls in tiny bikinis, then broke into a steady jog. The air smelled of sweaty bodies and expensive perfume, of the cloud of smog hovering over the city and the imminent tropic storm gathering over the nearby island.

I picked up in speed, jogging for at least an hour, before I stopped, irritated. Still no sign of Sofia, but I wouldn't give up, so I started moving and kept at it through the busy street, past imposing buildings and too much traffic. When I halted again, the sun had long set on the horizon in a million colors and the artificial light of the street lamps were casting a dim glow on the emptying streets. Running around like a stray cat had taken me nowhere. Maybe it was time to slow down and come up with a plan because my abilities didn't seem to be working here.

Burying my hands deep in my pockets, I strolled past what looked like a bar when I stumbled into something hard. Instinctively, I raised my hands to protect myself from the hazard, but nothing crashed into me. My gaze swept the area. Apart from a few young people having fun a few feet away and a few cars parked next to the sidewalk, there was nothing that could have hit me. I blinked and took another step forward, and another. And then it hit me again, almost sending me toppling backward.

"What the heck?" I murmured to myself. Was I running into an invisible shield? I had heard of them and knew they were created by magic, but I had never seen one strong enough to make me feel it. Maybe this would be my first encounter with something at least as strong as my demon blood.

I moved forward slowly but nothing happened. Figuring the barrier might not have been as powerful as I previously assumed, I shrugged it all off and crossed the street to resume my search. As soon as I zigzagged my way through the parked cars, Sofia's scent hit my nostrils. I inhaled deeply, feeling that smell of hers touch me deep inside. It was intoxicating and it made my head spin. Literally. I pressed my back against a parked car and took another whiff. It was still there. I wasn't dreaming.

I flipped my phone open and speed-dialed Cass's number. On the second ring, she picked up. "Found her. I'm going in," I whispered.

"No, you're waiting for—"

Cutting her off, I pushed my phone back inside my pocket and started down the street after Sofia's scent. A minute later I realized I wasn't alone.

"Where do you think you're going without us?" Cass said.

"How did you—" I peered at her, my irritation instantly evaporating. She was near her breaking point again. Soon the reaper in her would be forcing her to seek the nearest hospital.

"You forgot this little number." She waved her high-tech phone in front of my face, the one she had built to help her travel between earth and the dimensions of Hell until she received her full powers at eighteen.

I returned the grin. "Feel free to join the party. I'm glad you left the vampires at home."

"Who said I did?"

I followed her line of vision to the other side of the road where I had stood a few minutes ago. Of course, Aidan and Amber were there. They must have teleported, but they wouldn't have found me if Cass didn't reveal my exact whereabouts.

"What happened? Did you finally decide to get a sniffer dog?" Amber asked as she reached us.

"Don't mind her. She isn't always this insufferable," Aidan said. "Let's find the girl. Where is she?"

I pointed vaguely down the street. "Follow me. I hope you're fast because I'm not slowing down for you."

"You sound like my brother." Aidan laughed. Cass joined in, and I wondered whether she cracked up at his joke or the fact that she knew something he didn't. I sprinted through the dimly lit streets without paying attention whether the others followed behind. Sofia's scent grew stronger, enveloping my senses. My heartbeat sped up when it never did. No physical extortion ever bothered me—or provided much of a challenge—but this run did.

"We're there," I whispered, stopping in front of an old building not far from the beach.

"She's inside?" Amber's voice sounded hopeful.

I nodded.

"Well, what are we waiting for? Let's roll." Cass grabbed the large doorknob when Aidan held her back.

"You can't just barge in there. She's a mortal. You're going to scare her to death."

"I'll lure her out," I said.

"How?" Amber eyed me carefully.

"Just trust him," Cass whispered.

78

For a moment, the vampires fell silent, weighing my words. And then Aidan nodded.

I took a deep breath and pushed the door open. The entrance hall looked like no hotel I had ever seen with its faux-exotic theme in the form of carpets covering both the floor and the walls, and old lamps set up to illuminate the corners. Behind the counter, the night receptionist—a dark haired guy in his twenties—slept soundly. I inched closer and inspected his features, paying attention to the fine details because fine details were my specialty.

My tongue flicked over my lips as I concentrated. I pictured myself, from the snake tattoo across my entire chest and abdomen to my green eyes and dark hair, and then the picture slowly started to shift. My body became thinner and lost a few inches in height. The jeans and shirt I had been wearing all day changed into black slacks and a blue blazer with barely visible grease stains covering the front.

Even though I felt the same inside, I had shape shifted so many times before that I didn't need to look at myself in the mirror to know I looked exactly like the guy still sleeping in his chair. Time to make sure he'd stay that way. With my thumb and index finger, I touched his shoulder and pushed in the pressure point that would knock him out for a while, giving me enough time to persuade Sofia to leave her room. Without so much as a groan, his shape slumped into his chair and his head rolled back. I hid his thin body behind the desk.

My shoes made a squishing sound as I started up the stairs, following Sofia's scent to her room. I stopped to listen in front of her door. My demon ears picked up her shallow breathing. She was alone and asleep though something told me she was afraid of the pictures inside her mind. There were two options: either knock and risk waking up the other guests, or take her by surprise and not give her a chance to think clearly. Option two made sense to me so I picked the lock and opened the door slowly, then closed it behind me.

My eyes adjusted to the sudden darkness instantly and I looking around me. The room was small and tidy, the faintest scent of fried chicken hung in the air. Sofia lay on the bed to my right, pale legs peering from under the covers where her nightshirt had rode up her thighs. Her dark hair framed her face with high cheekbones and soft lips. I inched closer, my fingers reaching out to touch those lips, to see whether they were really as soft as I imagined them to be. My heart started to race as I pushed a thick strand of hair out of her face. She stirred with a soft moan, but didn't wake.

And then I remembered I had a job to take care of. I pulled my fingers back, wondering what was wrong with me. She was beautiful, all right, but I had seen my fair share of gorgeous girls. I shook my head at myself and leaned over her, covering my hand against her mouth as I switched on the night lamp.

80

Light flooded the room. Sofia's eyes flew open. Her blue gaze settled on me and I almost choked on my breath. Her eyes were of a sparkling blue as shimmering as the ocean hit by the first rays of sun. I stared at her, unable to utter a word, various emotions washing over me. She stared back, confused. The moment realization kicked in, the struggle began. She kicked hard, her leg hitting me in the chest. My grip around her tightened, my hand stifled her scream.

"Please listen. It's an emergency." My voice finally found its way out of my throat. I held her tight as I forced her to remain quiet. "I work at the reception downstairs. There's an important phone call for you. Do you remember me?" Her amazing eyes grew wide open as she nodded. I continued, "I knocked but you wouldn't answer. I'll remove my hand now and take a step back. Okay?"

She nodded again, so I pulled my hands back and took a few steps back. She eyed me carefully but didn't scream, which surprised me. The least I expected was a yelp.

"You said it's an emergency?" Sofia asked.

At the sound of her voice, I froze to the spot. Something happened—I could feel the change running through my body, like a tiny flicker of energy running through me for a brief second. Sofia's eyes grew wider. I drew in a deep breath to steady myself and focus on the illusion.

"Can you turn around or close your eyes so I can put something on then?"

81

I followed Sofia's demand with trepidation. Not only did I not like the idea of turning my back on her, I also wasn't keen on leaving her gorgeous legs out of sight.

"Is it Gael? Did something happen to him?" I heard her say as she slipped into her clothes. From the sound of it, it was a pair of jeans. Damn. Hopefully, they were tight ones.

"Well?" She tapped me on the shoulder and I turned to face her. The full impact of her eyes hit me. My mouth went dry. She raised her brows impatiently. "Do you understand me?"

I nodded. "The emergency is home."

"You mean my mother? What happened?" Panic crossed her face. So her mother was her weak point. I put on my most apologetic expression.

"I don't know any details."

"Right. Of course no one would tell you since you're not family."

She sure did all the work for me. "Please." I pointed at the door. She hesitated but followed me downstairs nonetheless. That was about as far as my plan went.

The reception stood as empty as before. "Where's the phone?" Sofia asked, looking around. The air crackled behind her and Amber appeared. I frowned. Sofia turned and followed my line of vision, surprise written on her face. "Where did you—"

"Just do me a favor and don't throw up all over me," Amber whispered as she wrapped her arm

82

around Sofia's shoulder. An instant later, they were gone. My concentration broke and my body turned back into my normal self. I opened the entrance door and slammed into Aidan. Cass regarded me coolly but didn't get involved.

"She teleported her out of here," I hissed.

"So?" Aidan shrugged. "Your job's done. We're taking over from here. Go home."

That was the deal, and yet the idea enraged me. "No." A growl gathered at the back of my throat.

"Whatever, mate. Suit yourself." Aidan held out his hand. "Need a lift?"

I grabbed it and regretted it almost instantly when a vacuum pulled me in. My stomach turned, my head began to spin. It was quickly over but the feeling of nausea remained. I bowled over, ready to empty the contents of my stomach, only then noticing a pretty brunette watching me from the corner of the room.

Chapter 8

The guy from the airport appeared right in front of me. My jaw dropped. I couldn't believe my eyes. Surely I must be dreaming. Given the events from the last few minutes, I was pretty sure my mind was playing a trick on me. I mean, one moment I had been standing in the hotel's reception area and the next I found myself in what seemed to be a hotel room or a living room designed by someone with exquisite taste. The hot guy bowling over in his quest to throw up all over the wooden floor completed the surreal feel of the situation. I was tempted to hurry over and wrap my arm around him, not to help but to just be near him, touch him, smell him. I rolled my eyes at myself. Desperate, all right. I averted my gaze for an instant only to turn back to him. From a few feet away, he was drop dead gorgeous with golden skin, smooth as marble, and that ripped look that no shirt could hide. His dark hair hung into his face, obscuring his eyes. But I could see his soft lips and for an instant I had the strong urge to just jump into his arms and crush my lips against his.

"What's wrong with people nowadays? First Amber couldn't keep her dirty thoughts to herself, and now this lot," a girl said, pointing at me. I turned to look at a pretty redhead with curls and ringlets bouncing around as she inched closer. "I'm Cass."

"Sofia." I pushed out my hand, then withdrew it again when my slow brain put two and tow together. If this wasn't a dream, I had just been kidnapped. *Kidnapped.*

"I never had dirty thoughts about Aidan," the girl next to me said, interrupting my trail of thought. She was the one who had appeared out of nowhere, wrapped her arm around me and then, a moment later when she dropped it again, I found myself in this room.

"Of course you did, mate." The redhead—Cass—snorted. "Need I remind you of that one time when you thought I was dating your guy and your brain just couldn't shut up about that steamy kiss you shared? Boy, I thought I'd need therapy for the rest of my existence."

"I've no idea what you're talking about," the brunette said. Annoyance crossed her delicate features that seemed quite familiar. I squinted and tilted my head to the side as I tried to remember where I had seen her before.

The blue-eyed guy standing next to the hot one from the airport held out his hand and I realized I had barely noticed him before. "I'm Aidan. And this is my girlfriend, Amber." He pointed at the brunette who now turned to face me.

"How did I get here?" I could slap myself for my stupidity. Any normal human with a working brain would've tried to run for the nearest exit. And yet here I was, talking to these people, wondering who they were and, most importantly, actually *liking* them. Talk about Stockholm syndrome big time.

"Relax," Cass said. "No one's kidnapped you. Yet. The big guy over there just might." She giggled and pointed at the luscious god I had just eyed up.

I raised my gaze to peer into the deep green eyes with hint of brown. His cheeks were slightly flushed, a hesitant smile played on his lush lips.

"I'm Thrain." He grabbed my hand, making my knees weak. My mouth opened and closed again, my mind went blank. I knew I had to say something, but I couldn't bring out a single word.

"Don't expect an answer any time soon," Cass said behind me.

"That's okay. We have all the time in this world," Thrain whispered so low I could swear he had talked to me. His voice dripped with something. It took me a while to realize it was the slightest hint of a promise. Surely, I couldn't be this stupid. These people probably kidnapped me and now wanted a ransom or something, and yet here I was, staring at a hot guy and wondering what it'd feel like to have his strong arms around me.

"Come on. We need to talk. And not about the hot guy." Cass pulled me down on the couch next to her and Aidan offered me a glass of water. I thanked him as I took it, but I was too clever to drink the liquid. No one would drug me. Cass continued, "Seriously, you're harder to find than truffles. You're probably wondering why you're here."

I shook my head. "Mostly, I'm wondering *how* I got here."

Cass took a deep breath and let it out slowly. "Since you're one of us, sort of, I see no reason to keep it from you. We beamed you from one place to another. You know, like Spook on *Star Trek*."

I raised my brows. "What?"

"*Star Trek?*" Cass regarded me incredulously. "You don't know *Star Trek*? You're kidding. Where have you been hiding? Under a stone? That series is so famous, we even have a fan club up in Heaven."

"We knocked you out and dragged you down here through a tunnel," Amber said. "Need more details?"

I shook my head. From up front, that girl was scary. And I'm not talking about the purple eyeshadow that emphasized the dark circles around her eyes—in fact, I was a huge fan of garish colors. She had that crazy, predatory look about her that would've made me cross the street to avoid her.

Thrain sat down next to me, his face inches away from my face as he leaned in, forcing me to face him. "Sofia, you're very special."

Cass's snort interrupted him. "With that crappy pickup line no wonder you're single."

Thrain raised his hand to stop her. His smoldering gaze remained focused on me. "No, let me finish. You have something that might save the life of one of our own."

"I don't understand." Which was the truth. Literally. I had trouble focusing on what he was saying already, what with those bulging arms and sensual lips, I didn't need him beating around the bush.

"Do you remember the TV show you watched a few days ago?" Cass asked. How did she know I watched it? My mind began to race in search for possible answers, and I nodded slowly unable to see where this was going. My gaze wandered to Amber who stood near the wall, quiet as a tomb. Then it dawned on me. Her straight, light-brown hair seemed a bit shorter, maybe because it was tied up in a ponytail. But her face was the same, minus the frightened expression I saw on TV. Cass snapped her fingers in front of my face, bringing me back to reality "Hey, she's not the scary one. Trust me, I'm the big deal here. You should see me in an hour or two when I'm not such a pretty sight."

"We need your help," Thrain said softly. I ran a hand through my hair as I tried to make sense of their words. They had told me their names, but they had yet to tell me who they really were because, right now, I was on the edge of believing everything in a situation that felt already surreal, like a dream from which I expected to wake up any minute.

His eyes really drew me in. I could gaze into them forever, lose myself inside that labyrinth of sparkling green intermingled with brown. I had never been one to fall quickly for a guy. Just look at Gael; we had been dating for six months, and I still hadn't gone past second base. And here I was, knowing this guy for all of two minutes, and I was already mentally choosing my bridal gown. Crazy, I know, but I couldn't help myself. And so I found myself saying the most stupid thing I could have said: "Sure. What do you want me to do?"

"Do you know who you are?" Thrain asked.

From all the questions, I had to admit I didn't see that particular one coming. "What?" I frowned. "Of course I do. I've known my name ever since my birth. It's even on my birth certificate."

"I'll show you something," Aidan said, motioning to Amber. She nodded and walked over to her bag to pull out a shirt, then tossed it my way.

I caught it in midair and touched the brown stains on the white material. "What is it?"

"Blood," Cass said. "To be more precise, my fiancé's blood."

"I'm sorry," I said, meaning it. Tears gathered in my eyes because it reminded me of my own loss. I would have loved to say something that could express how sorry I really was for her and how much I wished it were different. But no words could ever feel the void left behind.

Cass squeezed my hand. "Hey, I know how you feel. After losing your sister, I bet you wished you could bring her back."

"How do you know about my sister? How do you know so much of me?" My heart started to beat faster. The entire situation didn't make any sense.

She moistened her lips and for the first time I noticed the tiny freckles on her pale skin. "Let's just say I know where your sister is."

"She's alive?" I couldn't help the sudden hope rising inside me, only to die down like a blown out candle when I saw the pained expression on Cass's face.

"If you agree to save my brother, you can meet her, talk to her, say the goodbye you never got to say," Amber said.

Surprisingly, I didn't doubt her words. All my life I had known someone would be coming for me one day. I had also known they would want something only I could give, but I could never figure out what that was. I had no idea how I could help Cass's fiancé.

"The physical realm is not everything there is," Thrain said.

The crow popped into my mind and the darkness that kept beckoning to me in my dreams. I had seen pictures of things I didn't understand, of a cabin in the woods and an old woman who lived there, surrounded by herbs and animals. People had knocked on her door, asking for favors in a language I didn't understand—and yet, even though I didn't grasp the meaning of their words, I could feel the urgency, the hope and the trust they bestowed upon her. She had never denied anyone, just as I couldn't deny the people in this room. In my culture we recognized destiny and didn't run from it.

"Have you ever felt a strong urgency to pierce some needles into a doll?" Cass said. I shook my head. She cocked a brow. "Oh gosh, you're killing me. Not even once?" I shook my head more vigorously, wondering whether she actually meant it.

"You're a reborn voodoo priestess," Amber called out.

"Now that's preparing her for the big blow," Cass said. "Thanks for that, mate. Why didn't you just empty a bucket of ice-cold water over her head? I'm pretty sure that would've been less of a shock."

"A voodoo priestess." I rolled the words on my tongue tentatively, weighting them against my knowledge and beliefs. They sounded —right. In fact, so very right that it scared me. Something inside me clicked into place and I knew Cass was telling the truth.

Cass narrowed her gaze. "You don't need much persuasion, do you? Why's that?"

I shrugged. Maybe because she had a point. I didn't need other people to tell me what I was because my *babushka* had told me many times that my legacy was waiting for me. When my parents separated and my father moved to America, I stayed behind with my mother. My grandmother, who I called *babushka*, had taken care of me because my mother couldn't cope with the pain of losing her husband to another woman. For many years, she held on to the hope that he would return—until Theo was born and Mother finally accepted he'd never leave his new American family for what he left behind. It was during those years that Babushka told me stories about the Romanov family, and in particular a legend of how the seventh daughter of a seventh daughter would inherit the soul of a powerful witch. My mother married into the Romanov clan, but she was Babushka's sixth daughter. As far as I knew, I had only five elder siblings who died one after another in the harsh Siberian winter before I was born. I figured, maybe one of the miscarriages had been twins.

"I'm sorry." Cass gave my hand a quick squeeze.

"Before you ask, she can read your mind," Amber said, her eyes glinting with amusement. "So, if I were you, I'd be careful around her. So, no dirty thoughts, nothing about her dress style, and please don't encourage her to stay over because she does—a lot."

I nodded, thankful for the advice. But my mind had yet to comprehend the meaning of Amber's words. Or maybe I was just unwilling to believe it because no one could read someone else's thoughts. It wasn't possible.

"So you have absolutely no experience with voodoo?" Aidan asked. I shook my head because it was the truth. I had no *first hand* experience, which didn't mean my grandmother hadn't let me watch her fall into trance and perform the odd ritual. Of course I could've told them that I was eager to try—I had been all my life—but it didn't feel right. Yet. I wanted to find out who they were and what they could do first. Besides, something told me to wait before I revealed more about myself. Aidan tapped an impatient finger against his thigh. "Right. Cass, do you know anyone who can teach her?"

All eyes shifted back to the redhead, all but one pair. Thrain continued to stare at me. I moved in my seat uncomfortably, avoiding his probing gaze even though I could barely peel my eyes off of him. The way he seemed to take up the entire room, he made it impossible to focus on anything else. I moistened my lips only to regret it when his gaze followed the tip of my tongue. Cass tapped me on my shoulder, jerking me out of my thoughts. I turned to her, embarrassed that I had been so engrossed in my reflections I hadn't even heard her. "Sorry. What did you say?"

Cass rolled her eyes. "I said, what do you say to an all-inclusive trip to the Swiss Alps? If you're into snow and freezing to death, you might even enjoy it."

"We don't have time for skiing," Amber said.

"I know that," Cass snapped. "Give me some credit, will you? My aunt, Patricia, lives there and she's a Seer. She knows a lot about magic and stirring

93

into pots and all that. Might be a good start until we figure out what it takes to turn this lot into a proper priestess."

"I'm ready to go whenever you are," I whispered.

She shook her head and pointed behind her. The air around her seemed to move, carrying over a strange sound, like that of cracking wood. Staring was rude, and yet I couldn't look away as dark shadows erupted from her back, taking the shape of black wings. Cass threw her head back. Her eyes rolled in their sockets. When she peered at me, I could see they had changed color from green to pitch black, pain reflecting in them. Her skin turned darker until it resembled shiny coal. I flinched, not with disgust, but with fear. Whatever Cass was, I had seen it before, or so it seemed. The memory hovered at the back of my mind, begging me to remember, and yet I couldn't quite place the familiar sight. And then I remembered the pain searing through me. It was only a moment, but it left me perturbed, and more confused than before.

Thrain stood up and placed a soft peck on her forehead whispering, "Don't worry. I'll take care of her until you're back." Cass nodded and her mouth parted, revealing razor sharp teeth. I couldn't help but flinch. And in that instant, she disappeared right before my eyes.

"Are you okay?" Thrain asked me.

"Yes." My voice sounded surprisingly strong and resolute.

94

"She's one of the good guys." He reached out for my hand, then withdrew again as though he didn't know whether he had permission to touch me. I wished he hadn't stopped.

"I know that," I said softly. "I can feel it." And it was the truth. In my culture, there was a name for what Cass was—a *Giltinė*. A mixture of angel and demon, and a reaper of souls that could mean only one thing: death. Babushka had told me stories about a woman in white clothes with a never-fading green sprout in her hand. The touch of the sprout would put a human to an everlasting sleep. Granted, Cass's clothes couldn't be more colorful, but I figured even reapers might develop a sense for fashion. Babushka's stories made me believe I was truly seeing a being of Slavic mythology. I also knew I had nothing to fear, not before my time had come.

"Why don't you get some sleep while she's gone?" Aidan said. "She might take a while."

Thrain shook his head. "We can't stay here."

"Why not?" Aidan asked.

"Because this place is fishy. There's a reason why I didn't find her straight away."

"Like?"

Thrain regarded me. "Magic."

"You think someone's trying to stop us?" Amber inched closer and snuggled into Aidan's arms. For some reason I felt jealous of how natural she behaved. I wished I had someone I could feel so comfortable with.

"Maybe," Thrain said, hesitating. "Or maybe not. Either way, I'd rather not stay here. We might outnumber whoever's involved, but we don't know what we're dealing with. I say we wait for Cass at that forsaken place in Scotland. What was it called?"

"Inverness?" Aidan prompted. "The Lore Council's still looking for us. My house's the first place they'll suspect."

Thrain hesitated, thinking. "You're probably right. But the property's protected by magic, and you both can teleport. By the time someone gets in, you're already gone. What do you say?"

Aidan shifted to face Amber. I held my breath as I turned from them to Thrain and then back to them. Seriously, the way they stared at each other freaked me out. Their faces remained blank but something seemed to cross their pale features every now and then, and I wondered whether they could actually communicate with one another telepathically.

Amber nodded and jumped up. "Goody. I take her, you take him. Whoever's last is a lame duck." Grabbing my hand, I felt that push again and the weird sensation in the pit of my stomach returned. A groan escaped my throat as I closed my eyes and leaned into the comforting hand holding me tight. I heard what sounded like a light switch. A moment later, when I dared to look again, I was standing in the middle of a large room with modern furniture and a huge fireplace. The nausea forgotten, I turned to the window to look at the low moon casting a soft glow over the huge patch of greenery stretching behind the large bay windows. In Rio it had been night. Here, morning was about to break. We had just travelled thousands of miles, from South America to Europe, in just a few seconds.

"Is that—" My voice trailed off.

"Woods?" Amber laughed. "Uh-huh. I remember the first time I came here I couldn't stop staring."

I returned the smile. "Where I come from we have lots of green but it's usually covered by a huge layer of snow. This is magical. May I?" I pointed at the window. She nodded, so I inched closer and opened it wide to draw in a huge breath of air. It smelled delicious of earth and rain and damp wood. Mystical. With the time difference, I guessed it was about five a.m. Even tough I was tired from all the lack of sleep, the sun was about to rise, and I had no intention to miss my first sunrise in the Scottish Highlands.

The groan behind me told me Aidan and Thrain had just arrived. Judging from Thrain's pained expression and body language—him bowled over as if he was about to empty his stomach all over the floor, rasping for breath—I guessed he didn't enjoy it.

Thrain let out a string of curses. Talk about travel sickness. I smiled under my breath. Gael would never have let his guard down like that. Gael. In all the drama and excitement I had completely forgotten about my boyfriend. How could I possibly? What would he think when he found out I was gone?

"I need to make a phone call," I said.

Amber eyed me carefully. "To whom?

Her attitude didn't deter me. She was anxious that no one discovered our whereabouts. Though I had no idea what was going on, I somehow understood the magnitude of the situation and was okay with her brusque way. "My boyfriend." For some reason my gaze wandered instantly to Thrain as though to catch his reaction. He didn't say a word but a thin line formed on his forehead. It could be the result of his dizziness, which was obvious from the way he leaned against the couch, his hands clutching the chocolate brown material for dear life. Did I want him to be jealous? I pondered the thought for a moment, coming to the conclusion that I very much did.

Amber winked at Thrain. "Can't be the real deal if you're mentioning him only now."

I could feel the telltale heat of a blush scorching my cheeks. "It's sort of—"

The door burst open, interrupting my halfhearted attempt at providing a believable explanation. In the doorway stood a stunning blonde with glossy hair that framed her face with skin like porcelain and elfin features.

"Aidan?" She inched closer and grabbed him in a tight hug, laughing. "Oh, my gosh. I thought I'd never see you again."

"You mean you *hoped* you'd never see me again." He laughed as she punched his arm playfully.

"You're such an idiot. How could you even say that?" She pushed him away and turned to Amber,

98

regarding her for a long moment, before she wrapped her long arms around her. She was so tall, she looked like she just stepped out of a fashion magazine. Even though I had no idea who she was, the blonde had such an infectious smile I felt myself laughing with her and savoring what seemed to be a surprise reunion.

"Sofia, this is Clare. Clare, meet Sofia," Aidan said. I opened my mouth to speak, but he cut me off. "Where's Kieran?"

Clare let out an exaggerated sigh. "Don't even ask. Your dear brother's been gone for two weeks now and he wouldn't tell me where. But apparently it's a job that could solve all of our problems."

"That sounds like trouble," Amber said.

"Right?" The blonde laughed. "That's what I told him but he wouldn't listen. Anyway—"

"We're the odd ones out," Thrain whispered in my ear. I felt something wafting from him, making me wonder what it was. Maybe pure sex appeal. The guy oozed sensuality. Strange words echoed in my ear in a language I didn't understand. The room started to spin slowly, then faster and faster. The others became a blur that merged into one shapeless heap. Through the huge cloud enveloping me, I felt Thrain's hand tighten around my wrist. His voice came from far away. "Are you okay? Sofia? Something's wrong with her." I opened my mouth to tell him that I was all right, but he needed to remove his hand from my arm because his fingers were singeing my skin. Literally. I peered in horror at what looked like huge blisters bubbling like boiling water right under my skin. A shriek escaped my throat. I pulled my hand back but his grip didn't loosen. The room continued to spin so fast, it reminded me of the carousel I rode as a child. The spinning sensation had been the most painful and frightening experience I ever had. Then the flattering of hundreds of wings began again, drumming against my skull. I winced.

"Shush." Thrain pulled me against his chest.

"What's wrong?" a female voice asked.

"No idea," he whispered.

Something cold touched my temple. I leaned into it, welcoming the cooling sensation against my feverish skin. Thrain let me go to hold a glass of water to my lips, begging me to take slow sips. And then the spinning and strange noises stopped. The others had gathered around me and stared at me like I was a freak, which I probably was. I peered at them, probably just as surprised as they were.

"What happened?" Amber asked.

I shook my head, signaling that I didn't know. But I had a theory, even if it was an implausible one. My powers were claiming me, urging me to take the plunge before it was too late. The sudden onset of fear threatened to choke me as I looked out the window at the crow perched on the low branch of a thick tree. It cawed three times before it took off again.

Chapter 9

In the end I decided not to call Gael but my mother in Siberia. It was late afternoon there, meaning I disrupted her work, so the conversation was brief to the point of painful. She didn't buy into my explanation of meeting some friends from college and eloping to Europe. Her interpretation of my disappearance was that things between Gael and me were moving too fast, and while she didn't express disapproval of my actions, she did remind me of Gael's wealth at least twice. Money rules the world—how could I argue with that? And yet I could feel the change inside and all around me. Where I was heading, money had no value.

But that I kept to myself.

The sun had risen over Scotland in thick streaks of yellow and gold. White, fluffy clouds hovered in the sparkly blue horizon, promising a sunny day. Yet I could feel the rain in my bones. Another an hour or two and Mother Nature would be opening the floodgates. Somehow I looked forward to the downpour that would replenish the ground with moisture.

"Are you cold?" Thrain asked behind me. Smiling, I turned to see him in the backdoor of the kitchen, holding a jacket. He inched closer and draped it around my shoulders, then gave them a quick rub as though to warm me up. "May I?" When I nodded, he sat down on the cold stairs. His naked arm almost brushed my sleeve. Even though I couldn't feel his skin, my whole body began to tingle. His green gaze made me nervous, so I looked away as I inhaled the clean scent of nature and—sandalwood, myrrh, crushed minerals. I knew that particular smell wafted from him.

Thrain spoke first. "You never told us why you accepted this so easily. I mean, every other woman would have called us crazy and run for a mile."

I moistened my lips as I considered my words. How much could I tell him? He was a pretty face, all right, but a pretty face didn't exactly equal trustworthy. "Let's just say I've heard a few stories about this world."

"Fair enough. You don't know me. Why would you tell me anything?" He bobbed his head, but I could hear the disappointment in his voice.

"I'm ready to fulfill my life's purpose, Thrain," I whispered.

"Aren't you a bit too young to have figured out your life's purpose already?"

"You're never too young, only too blind to see it." I stared at my jeans and the soda stains now faded from all the washing. My gaze searched his. "What are you? I mean all of you. The blonde girl, Clare, she said she had to rest because the sun was rising soon. Amber and Aidan can move to places in the blink of an eye. And you—" I stopped to catch my breath, wondering why I was blurting out all those questions to this guy. He mustn't think me naïve. I had knowledge but just needed to cast the characters into the right play.

A soft breeze rustled the leaves in the trees. The woods stretched as far as the eye could see, beyond the tall fence hidden behind rosebushes, up to the mountains in the distance. The grass stirred softly beneath our feet. Thrain hesitated for a long moment, as if unsure whether to answer my unspoken question. Eventually, his gaze connected with mine. A deep furrow had formed between his brows, but even with this imperfection, he didn't look human. His skin was too evenly tanned and too smooth, the shape of his jaw too perfect. I smiled and rubbed a hand over the stains on my jeans. What was I doing here with this guy in a world I didn't belong? And yet a voice inside my head told me my old life was over. As if to give credence to my belief, a black crow swooned past our heads and perched down on a nearby tree. I glanced at the bird just to see whether it was the same one as before, then turned back to Thrain. The soft breeze blew a stray stand of hair into my face. He leaned in and flicked it behind my ear. His fingers felt soft where he touched my skin, leaving behind a tingling sensation. It was almost the same burn as before when I had lost any sense of reality, but not as strong and far more pleasant.

"Someone I know made a huge mistake of not telling someone she loved the truth about her," Thrain whispered. "I don't see a reason why there should be secrets between us. Do you?" I shook my head. He took a deep breath, then continued, "Clare, Aidan and Amber are vampires, though Aidan and Amber don't feed on blood. Cass is a fallen angel turned reaper due to a curse. And I was created in Hell as a high-ranked demon. My abilities involve tracking and shape shifting."

I gulped, considering his words. My gaze searched his eyes for an sign that he was lying. There was none. He seemed as earnest as one could be. Russian folklore is full of demons and shape shifters. They're usually said to lure one into anything from temptation to death, from signing away one's soul to sacrificing one's first born. Babushka had taught me to be the superstitious kind. However, she also taught me not to fear every creature of the night. Even if I wanted to be scared of him I knew I had no reason to be. He didn't mean me any harm.

"You seem pretty cool about it." Thrain raised his brows.

"Where I come from meeting a demon isn't the worst thing that could happen to you." I smiled. His brows furrowed. "I'm originally from Siberia. A majestic yet scary place." I gestured around me as though that might send the picture inside my mind straight into his brain so he'd know what I meant. Unfortunately, that didn't happen. I laughed at his confused expression. "Where I grew up, everyone's superstitious. But what we feared the most were the harsh winters and lack of food and losing a loved one to the fever."

"I'm sorry." He squeezed my hand gently.

"No, don't be." I smiled, lost in my memories. "It's a beautiful place, probably the most beautiful place in the whole world, but also one of the most dangerous. In late spring, when the snow recedes, we often found missing animals and sometimes even people thawing in the warm sun. It's a gruesome sight."

"I can only imagine."

"There's so much snow up there, everything's of a perfect white. As a child I often thought I was in Heaven walking on fluffy clouds," I said. He looked at me the whole time while I recalled key moments of my childhood. He was a good listener, giving his inputs at the right time, making me feel relaxed. He was so different from Gael, who was never really interested in my past. "You should visit one day." I added. "Just make sure to put on a few layers of clothes."

He laughed and touched my hand. "Awesome advice. It might come in handy sometime. Since I've always had issues with popularity, what with infusing fear coming with the job description of a demon, I might just consider moving there."

I opened my mouth to ask whether he was serious, but Thrain cocked his head and pointed to the inside of the house. My ears strained to listen. An instant later, Cass stood in the doorway. Her skin was flushed with a glow to it, as was her red hair. She was wearing a summer dress now, white with tiny blue flowers, and a thick, orange sweater on top of it. What looked like combat boots perfected her outfit. The entire assemble looked good on her. In fact, after realizing what she was I couldn't imagine her in strappy sandals or high heels.

"Took you longer than before," Thrain said. Even if it weren't for the tight lines around his mouth, I could feel him stiffen beside me. My curiosity awakened instantly.

"Relax," Cass said, slumping down beside me. "There's plenty of time."

"How is he?"

Cass shrugged. "Obviously, still dead. Why do you keep asking?" She leaned forward to peer at him. He turned away.

"Maybe I was hoping for a miracle," Thrain whispered.

"Here's our miracle." Cass pointed at me. A few awkward seconds passed. For the umpteenth time, I

106

wondered what was going on between them and whether they had some sort of mind-thing keeping their real conversation hidden from prying ears.

Cass raised her brows, grinning. "Scotland, the land of mystery? I thought we agreed on the Swiss Alps."

"It was a spur of the moment decision," Thrain said. Was Cass the one having the last word and he expected a confrontation now? If he did, it never came. Cass got up and wiped a hand over her dress as though to remove any dust.

"Whatever. We're leaving now. Patricia will need time to teach her. The vampires will stay here for...research purposes." She gazed at me, and I knew research purposes involved finding out whatever they could about being a voodoo priestess. It seemed they knew even less than I did. It might just be the right time to reveal that I wasn't the complete beginner they believed me to be. With every breath I took, something seemed to fall into place, like a puzzle, and memories kept flooding my mind. Even though they seemed like distant dreams, I knew they spoke of a past that had once been my life. I needed more time to make sense of those memories, to study them, to find clues that would help me trigger everything there was to know, so I kept my secret to myself.

I touched Cass's elbow and pointed a few feet away. She nodded and let me draw her aside. Harboring any hope that Thrain didn't have the ability or heightened sense of hearing to tune into our conversation was stupid. And yet I wanted to believe it because I had been meaning to talk to her in private ever since I remembered having seen her before.

She raised her brows. "What's wrong?"

"I need to talk to you about something."

"Can it wait?"

I shook my head, slightly hesitating. The truth was it could wait. It had for six months now.

Cass squeezed my hand. "Once we're at Patricia's, okay? This place isn't safe, what with Aidan's exes trying to kill the new missus and the Lore court standing in their way." She rolled her eyes, then smiled. "I promise I'll answer all your questions about your sister later."

Sensing that was more than I could even dream of only recently, I nodded and mouthed a thank you.

"Wait here," Cass continued. "I'll be right back. Just need to give a few instructions before your big adventure begins, otherwise this lot is lost without me."

I stared after her as she returned to the house, her pace bouncing, her hair swaying as though she had more energy than she could ever utilize. It was strange seeing her on such a high when only a few hours ago she looked pale and fatigued.

"It's weird, isn't it?" Thrain asked.

I nodded, turning to regard him. "You said she took longer this time."

"Yes." A sparkle of worry appeared in his eyes. "She's a reaper now with the kiss of death on her

108

back. Soon, it might claim her forever unless—" He took a deep breath and smiled.

"Unless I help her," I finished for him. He didn't respond, which was fine by me. He didn't need to say it. "What is it she wants me to do?"

"I don't know, Sofia. My job was to find out your whereabouts. Everything else is just a huge question mark. I doubt even Cass knows what you're actually supposed to do."

"It's a huge deal, isn't it? And failure isn't an option," I whispered. His green gaze enveloped me, drawing me closer to him. I wished he would just wrap his arms around me to tell me everything would turn out all right. But he didn't. Instead, his eyes seemed to caress me as they brushed over my face. They seemed to talk to me, tell me of something I didn't know. That we were too different and yet we were meant to meet, meant to experience this adventure of a lifetime together. I shook my head at the strange thoughts in my mind, wondering why I was interpreting so much into beautiful eyes and a warm gaze. Obviously, we liked each other, but I had liked a few guys before him. The only thing out of the ordinary was that he wasn't human.

A strong breeze scattered the leaves on the ground. I picked one up and held it between my thumb and middle finger, rubbing the frail surface, marveling at how thick it seemed. Ever since moving to New York, I realized I had been growing out of tune with nature. City life wasn't me. This display of untouched nature was what I envisioned for myself, where I wanted to live. Yet I knew I couldn't have it for a few more years, until I made it as a musician and could settle down wherever my heart would take me. I dared a glance toward Thrain, wondering where his heart might be.

"Yo, ready to go?" Cass yelled from the door, startling me. I nodded and took a step forward, confused. The others seemed to just move to places, something they called 'teleporting.' Cass was something entirely else though. I had yet to see what she could do. For a moment, I pictured huge wings sprouting out of the back of her sweater, then a wink and she'd be motioning Thrain and me to hold on for dear life as she flew us over the Scottish Lowlands, past England and France, toward the Swiss Alps. Grinning at my own stupid thoughts, I pushed the ridiculous image out of my head.

"You couldn't possibly think any girl in her right mind would ever do that wearing a skirt. I'm not keen on putting my cream pie on display, you know." Cass pulled out her phone. I thought she needed to make a phone call or something, until she started punching on the keys like a maniac and the air began to crackle. My eyes widened, though I wished they wouldn't because I probably made a complete fool of myself.

Cass pointed at the air, grinning. "Please, step right through."

"Through where?" I asked.

"Give me your hand."

I grabbed her outstretched palm and took a tentative step forward. The air crackled some more as Cass's left side disappeared. She looked as though she had been cut in half, which freaked me out.

"It's a portal," I muttered, feeling even more stupid because I should have known if people could teleport from one place to another, they sure could open portals to take them to places. Cass walked through and I followed behind, closing my eyes just in case this sort of traveling would trigger the same nausea as teleporting. A freezing wind engulfed my body, making me shiver. After counting to five, I opened my eyes again and squinted against the glaring brightness, and for a brief moment I thought I was back home in Siberia.

Chapter 10

The greenery of the Scottish Highlands was gone. Instead, I found myself surrounded by snow. And when I say surrounded, I mean lots of it, as in everywhere. If it wasn't for the bright sun and the rising mountains in the distance, I could have sworn we were back home in Siberia, not least because it was just as cold. Shivering against the thin material, I wrapped Thrain's jacket around me and wondered whether he would follow. A moment later, he stepped through the portal and I breathed out, relieved.

"Damn. This thing's malfunctioned again," Cass said, shaking her phone about as though that might help.

Thrain's green eyes gleamed as he shot me an amused look. I smiled back. The way the sun reflected on his tan skin made my heart skip a beat. My fingers itched to touch him. But touching wasn't an option.

Not when we both had a mission to fulfill and I had absolutely no excuse for reaching out to him.

"Need help?" he asked Cass.

"Why would I?" she snapped. "I *designed* this thing, remember?"

He held up a hand, grinning. "Hey, chill. I just thought—"

"Don't think. Just be a pretty face." She walked away, huffing and scoffing at the phone.

"She doesn't mean it," Thrain whispered. "Ever since Dallas died, she's been a bit cranky."

"Who could blame her?" I wanted to tell him that I could emphasize with Cass because I knew what it was like to lose a loved one. I opened my mouth to speak, then closed it again as he grabbed my hand and gave it a light squeeze as though he could somehow sense it.

"Hold on to me," Thrain said, wrapping his arm around my waist. "We wouldn't want you to slip. Or worse—turn into an ice cube."

Grateful, I leaned into him to soak up the warmth emitted by his skin. Even though he was wearing short sleeves, he wasn't even shivering while the cold was slowly creeping into my bones. Soon, I wouldn't be able to keep my teeth from clattering. We caught up with Cass. Her head was still bowed over the phone and grim lines had formed around her mouth.

"Hey, boss, maybe we should call the customer service helpline," Thrain said, winking at me.

Cass rolled her eyes. "Aren't you hilarious?"

I didn't get their joke until Thrain explained, "She worked in customer service. We used to crack jokes about her customers, and in particular about those who couldn't figure out how to use a phone." I looked into his eyes, interested. A reaper working in a nine to five job? I never expected that. He pulled me closer until I could feel his warm breath on my temple as he spoke. "Anyway, I wish she could stop being so stubborn and let me have a look. If that thing doesn't work soon, we might end up having to think about sleeping quarters for the night because there's no way she'll give up."

"I heard that," Cass yelled. Her voice echoed in the distance. The snow crackled beneath our feet. I watched in horror as a huge chunk of snow broke off from one of the mountains and rained down the pit.

"Not only will we freeze to death, we'll also die buried beneath a huge layer of snow," I whispered.

Thrain laughed. "I didn't know you were psychic as well. Beauty and talent, now that's quite a catch."

I found myself laughing with him as his words kept replaying in my mind. Forget the talent remark, he found me beautiful. I had heard that one before, but coming from him it actually meant something. I really hoped he meant it and it wasn't the usual pick up line he told every girl.

"Are you two courting or what? Come on, we haven't got all eternity," Cass yelled.

"For a moment I was inclined to believe we did, Cass, because that's how long this is taking," Thrain answered. Cass grinned back and motioned us to hurry up. I peered at them, wondering how long they had been friends that they felt so at ease around one another. A pang of jealousy grabbed hold of me, not because I didn't like them to be friends, but because I wished I had known Thrain for so long. I didn't doubt for a second once this mission was over, he'd return to his world and I'd return to mine. I had known him for all of five minutes and already the thought of never seeing him again was unbearable.

We reached Cass and walked through another portal. This time I didn't close my eyes. I expected to see something like a tunnel—in fact, anything that might resemble a wormhole or a door surrounded by kaleidoscope colors—but apart from the static in the air that made my hair rise, there was nothing. One moment we were on one side, and the next we were on the other. I scanned the new area, surprised to see yet more snow. I wondered whether Cass's phone had malfunctioned again and the portal had spit us out in the same spot as before until I saw smoke rising from a chimney in the distance.

"Well done, Cass," Thrain said. His praise sounded genuine. Cass beamed and punched some more on her phone until the hip-high snow cleared away, leaving a clear path in front of us that led to the miniature of a medieval mansion with beautiful, little towers and bay windows. I craned my neck to get a better view. The sun reflected in the thick glass, making it impossible to peer inside, but I could make out pink curtains with lace and flower details. The wooden door looked massive; I doubted two men would be able to kick it in. In New York, it would cost a fortune.

"Wow," Thrain whispered. I thought he was just as impressed as I was until he continued, his words baffling me. "Poor Patricia. This place is a fortress indeed." It didn't look like one to me. More of a nice holiday resort, and an inviting one at that, what with the wooden sign advertising MAGIC CUPCAKES.

Cass knocked on the huge brass lion doorknocker. A moment later, a girl around my age opened. Her smile froze on her lips as she peered from Cass to Thrain and then back to Cass, paying me no attention at all. I stared at her red hair, milky complexion and the stunning green eyes. If it wasn't for her larger bosom, rounder hips and less freckles, I could have sworn she was Cass's twin.

"You're kidding me. What do I own the pleasure of yet another visit from you?" the girl asked. Her voice betrayed her surprise, but also wariness. Her eyes sparkled, though I wasn't sure whether with joy or malice.

"Oh, shut up, Patty. Let us in. We're freezing to death in this forsaken part of the world," Cass said, pushing past her. "It's not even on *Google Maps*."

116

I hesitated, unsure whether to follow, until the girl heaved an exaggerated sigh and motioned us to come in.

"Thank you," I mumbled.

"I'm Patricia," she said, closing the door behind us. "And you are?"

"Oh, for crying out loud. You're a Seer. You should know who she is." Cass rolled her eyes and slipped out of her coat, tossing it toward Patricia. "And since we're talking jobs and skills here, when we last met you could have told me Dallas was about to die. I know I would've done it if the roles were reversed."

"I'm sorry. The pictures in my head weren't clear enough to interpret the message," Patricia said uncomfortably.

"Whatever. Water under the bridge, mate. This is Sofia. She's helping out." Cass grabbed my arm and led me into a huge kitchen with walls made of stone and huge hearths. I looked around, sweat starting to pour down my back from the heat. Fires were lapping at wood logs hungrily. On the left side were large trays with pastries, muffins and cakes, their delicious aroma tickling my nose. My stomach rumbled in response, reminding me I hadn't eaten in a long time. I wondered whether it'd be rude to ask whether I could buy something. Thank goodness I didn't need to. Patricia set desert plates on the gigantic oak table to our right and pointed at the chairs. Cass slumped down and I followed suit, albeit shyly. Pushing his chair closer, Thrain sat down next to me, his arm brushing mine.

"You're still mad, aren't you?" Cass said, eyeing the tray of hot muffins Patricia pulled out of an oversized oven.

"What do you think?" she said through gritted teeth. "Your boyfriend almost killed me."

"Get a grip, Patty. It was an accident. I told you, like, a million times it was that curse of yours that made him want to strangle you when you opened to door and stepped out." Cass turned toward me and rolled her eyes as though I knew what she was talking about.

"Please, help yourself. And whatever you do, don't open the kitchen door. My curse says I mustn't leave this house, or else I'm dead. Last time, Cass forgot that tiny detail. We wouldn't want another *accident.*" Patricia shot Cass a meaningful glare before placing a plate with muffins in front of us, then went about pouring us huge mugs with a clear liquid that looked like water but smelled much sweeter. I took a tentative sip and let it roll over my tongue. It tasted sweet and flowery, and almost as good as the hot blueberry muffins.

"Elderberry," Thrain said. "I loved it as a kid."

I forced myself to swallow down the chunk in my mouth before replying. "It's great. Where did you learn to make this?"

Patricia took the seat opposite from me and shrugged. "I didn't. It's my curse. I'm stuck in this

118

place forever—or until the guy I'm meant to be with turns up."

"Since you can't even find this place on Google Maps, she'll probably have to go with forever," Cass said.

Patricia nodded grimly.

I placed my second, half-eaten muffin aside, though not out of reach since I very much intended to finish it. My cheeks turned hot before I even uttered the thought that bothered me ever since meeting Cass's aunt. "Sorry if I sound rude but you look like you're the same age."

Patricia grinned, and for the first time I noticed the tiny dimples in her chubby cheeks. I had thought her pretty, but smiling she was downright gorgeous. She ran a hand through her red mane. "Well, it's a complicated story. See, she's Lucifer's daughter." She pointed at Cass, who nodded. I felt my eyes widen but didn't comment. Patricia continued, "Like Lucifer, I'm a fallen angel, which makes him my brother because we share the same creator." She raised her gaze to the sky. I followed her line of vision, almost expecting the ceiling to burst open so we would catch a glimpse at Heaven. Of course, nothing happened.

"Get on with it, Patty," Cass said, drumming her nails on the table.

"Don't rush me. When do I ever get to talk to people, who actually know what I'm talking about?" She beamed at me. I didn't want to point out that I had no idea what she was going on about. Instead, I let her continue. "Anyway, I wasn't part of the plan. I mean, Heaven and Hell have two Seers already. But some moron invented the legend of three Seers, so for thousands of years everyone who passed into Heaven kept asking to see the third Seer, which really started to piss off the creator to the point that He decided to make a third eighteen years ago. Cass was born a day later, which makes us the same age. You probably have a million questions now."

I raised my brows, my mind still churning the details. Yep, I had lots of questions, but they had nothing to do with her. What did God look like? What was He like? Did every deceased soul get to talk to Him?

"Any questions? Don't be shy," Patricia said.

I strained my mind to come up with something that involved her and was very proud of myself when it did. "How were you created exactly?"

Patricia tapped a finger against her chin, thinking. "Uh, can't really remember. Must have slipped my mind. Anything else you wanna know?"

"What's God like?" I blurted out.

"Can't tell you," Patricia said.

I frowned. "Why not?"

She waved her left hand about. "Because we have rules and I'm not breaking them."

"Fair enough." I nodded, slightly disappointed. I mean, what was the big deal? She could at least give me a hint or two.

120

"You'll meet Him soon enough," Patricia whispered.

My head shot up. "What?"

"She's an idiot," Cass said, patting my hand. I regarded Patricia intently, but she turned away, hiding the expression on her face. My heart started to hammer in my chest. A Seer's someone who can foretell the future. I wondered whether she had just made a general remark or whether she saw my imminent death. Now that wasn't a promising outlook.

"She's actually the second most useless Seer I've ever met," Cass said, pouring herself more elderberry juice.

"Who's the most useless?" Thrain asked, amused.

"My aunt Krista. That lot couldn't predict the future if her life depended on it." Cass downed the glass in one big gulp and placed it back on the table. Her face turned dead serious, and I knew she was about to disclose why we came here. "Hey, Patty, what do you know about voodoo?"

Patricia blinked, taken aback. "What I've seen on TV, like piercing needles into a doll and falling into a trance with your eyes rolling back while talking with a weird voice in an ancient language."

Whoa, was that what would happen to me? I swallowed past the sudden lump in my throat. I thought being a witch meant brewing the odd love potion and speaking out a curse or two.

121

"That's not voodoo. It's called being possessed," Thrain said, still grinning.

"Oh." She nodded. "Right. Okay, then it's just the needles and the doll. And I remember something about chicken and blood, but that's gross."

Cass smirked. "And there I thought you might actually know something *useful*, like how to help a voodoo priestess get in touch with her powers."

"Is she one?" Patricia jumped up from her seat and walked around the table, stopping behind me. I felt her smooth hands on my shoulders, then on my cheeks and on my shoulders again. "I can feel her powers. She has been marked."

I held my breath, waiting for her to reveal more, but she remained quiet.

"By what? And shouldn't you have seen that the moment she entered your property?" Cass asked, impatiently.

Patricia's hands remained glued to my shoulders as she whispered, "By something very powerful." I felt Thrain's sudden tension. It passed on to me as though we were the same being. Words unspoken hovered at the back of my mind. I knew they were his, I could almost grasp their meaning and yet they kept slipping my perception.

"Could you be more specific?" Cass asked, irritated.

Patricia shook her head. "That's about as far as my powers go. Ask me in a few days when I turn eighteen and I might be able to help more."

122

Cass scoffed. "That's awesome news, particularly since we don't have any time to spare. Dallas is dead in less than a week unless we can figure out how to unleash her powers."

"Give me some credit," Patricia snapped, her eyes sparkling. "At least I can tell you *something*. What was it again you can do?" Someone definitely had a short temper. She looked so pissed off, I almost expected her to start smashing dishes. I peered at Thrain, my gaze begging him to intervene so disaster wouldn't unfold, but he just leaned back, grinning. Something in his eyes triggered a memory in me—darkness and the presence of something unnatural and scary, a cold sensation, then searing pain.

"I know what marked me," I heard myself say softly. All eyes turned on me. For the first time, I saw surprise written on Cass's face. I moistened my lips, uncomfortable with all the attention.

"You do?" Thrain prompted. His thigh brushed mine under the table, making any sort of concentration on the topic at hand impossible. Tiny jolts of electricity ran through me, wandering up and down my body. I had the strong need to touch him. Instead of giving in, I pulled away and crossed my legs, putting a few inches of distance between us. He frowned as though he knew I was uncomfortable with the proximity between us. Then again, I was probably reading too much into his expression.

"My—" I hesitated, considering my words because the word 'boyfriend' didn't quite feel right "—

Gael took me to see a fortuneteller. I think something happened, but I'm not sure."

And then I went about recalling my experience with Madame Estevaz. When I finished, Cass asked me to start again without leaving out any details. The huge frown on her forehead told me she was just as confused.

"So, when you woke up you couldn't remember a thing?" Thrain asked for the umpteenth time. I nodded. He smirked. "Why don't I like the sound of that?"

"Did you notice anything out of the ordinary when you woke up? Anything you didn't understand, anything that had you confused?" Patricia asked.

I bit my lip as I tried to remember, but my mind remained blank. "Don't think so."

"Take your time," she said, walking around the table and sitting back in her chair. "Even if it might've seemed irrelevant at that time, it could mean something."

I rubbed the sole of my left shoe over the stone tiles as I went through what happened after meeting Madame Estevaz. "Gael was there. I thought I saw something in his eyes, like a black shadow. A moment later, it was gone, but I think I saw it before." I moistened my lips and brushed my hand over my jeans, almost expecting the others to laugh and tell me I was being silly. Thrain wrapped his hand around mine and gave it a light squeeze as though to encourage me.

124

"Did you say 'black shadow'?" Cass shot Thrain a quizzical look.

I nodded. "Yes. Why?"

"Does he have eerie black eyes and dark hair?" Thrain asked. I didn't think he was serious until he cocked a brow.

"Oh, that was a real question." I shook my head. "No. Just brown eyes and light brown hair."

Cass's face dropped. "There goes my lead."

"We have another," Thrain said. "It's clear Madame Estevaz marked her. Let's see what she was really up to."

Chapter 11

I was slowly getting the hang out of this portal traveling. In fact, I felt like a natural, just walking through with not even a need to blink any more. After saying goodbye to Patricia and letting her hug me tight with what I swear were tears in her eyes, I returned to Rio de Janeiro. I wasn't sure where Madame Estevaz was, but apparently people knew her well. After half an hour waiting on a park bench, Thrain returned to let Cass and me know he had found her. So Cass opened yet another portal. An instant later, I found myself standing in front of the old house with the clean front yard and the peeling plaster. Thrain signaled us to stay behind him as he knocked. When no one answered, he shot us a glance over his shoulder and tried the door. It opened with a long creak.

"Anyone home?" Cass called out. I held my breath to listen for any sounds, but nothing stirred. Not even the chicken and pigs, I heard the last time I visited, made any sound.

"Something's wrong," Thrain whispered, pushing me behind him. I pressed my palm against the low of his back, feeling his muscles tensing beneath the thin material of his shirt.

Cass scoffed. "How did you figure that one out, Sherlock Holmes?"

As I followed them in, my gaze wandered to the mess that hadn't been here before. Dried herbs and broken ornament had been strewn all over the place. The papers, which had covered the wall above the heart to hide the chipped paint, had been torn to shreds. The mirror near the door had been smashed into hundreds of pieces. There was a plate with food on the table, as if someone got up quickly and didn't get the chance to finish a meal. The dismantled head of a ragdoll stared at me from the floor, its dark eyes were wide open, filled with accusation. That freaked me out because I knew it was just a doll.

I frowned in horror as I tried to make sense of what could possibly have happened. And then I noticed there was something in the air. A dark presence. Waves of—

"Chaos," Thrain said, taking a deep breath. His eyes glazed over, his mouth stood slightly open. I peered at Cass only to see her expression was similar.

"Pain," she whispered.

VOODOO KISS

My hand still pressed against Thrain's back, I could feel his excitement washing over me, making me feel something I had never experienced before. An ecstasy that reminded me of a reunion with a long lost friend or lover, leaving behind a strong need for more. And yet I knew this woman hadn't experienced a happy reunion. She was dead. I could feel it in my bones, as if she had been a kindred spirit and magic connected us.

I pulled my hand back quickly and bolted out the door and around the house, stopping only to throw up into a nearby bush. The nausea together with the relentless heat of the sun made me dizzy, but emptying my stomach felt surprisingly good, as though it would cleanse me from that sick sensation of enjoyment stemming from someone else's suffering.

"Are you okay?" Thrain said, rubbing my back.

I held up a hand as I leaned forward, my mind begging him to go away. I had no reason to be surprised. I mean, he had told me he was a demon and demons thrived on other people's pain. Even though I didn't like what I had just experienced, the initial shock was already starting to wear off. I wiped a hand over my mouth and turned to face him.

"I'm sorry you had to see that," he said softly. His gaze searched mine, his eyes probing to find out what I was thinking of him. I let him squirm and wonder as I took a minute to think about it. The knowledge of what caused him pleasure didn't lessen my attraction to him. He was still someone I hoped to get to know to see where it might take us. Maybe he sensed my thoughts and emotional undercurrents because his lips stretched into a smile and he held out his hand. I grabbed it, albeit reluctantly, but didn't budge from the spot when he tried to pull me away.

"No," I said. "I want to know what happened to her."

He hesitated. "Trust me, you don't. It's not a pretty sight." I caught his glimpse behind me and followed his line of vision, past a fence leading into an overgrown garden. I started in that direction with him behind me, my breath coming in short, ragged heaps. If he tried to stop me, I didn't hear it. My heart began to hammer loud and hard a moment before I stepped through the gate into the garden with herbs and wild flowers and heavy branches hanging from a weeping willow. Right under them was a paved space, a perfect circle with stones building a border about ten inches in height. A ritual place—I knew it because I had seen something like this in my reoccurring dreams and visions ever since I was born.

My hands shook as I kneeled down to touch the puddle of blood that had stained the stones a deep red, my gaze wandering past the pair of worn slippers to the old woman lying on her back in the middle of the circle. Her eyes were wide open, the expression on her aged face showed horror and fear. Her hands were tied and pressed against her chest as though she had tried to protect herself. Right under her chin was a thin cut crusted with dried blood. Bile rose in my throat. For once I was thankful I had skipped a lot of meals lately.

"Shush, it's okay. She didn't suffer." Thrain's hands drew slow circles on my back. I knew he was lying. He small incisions all over her body indicated whoever had killed her had ensured a long and painful death.

I got up and wiped my hands on the back of my jeans. "Get me out of here." My voice came low and hoarse, choked with emotion. I could feel something wet and cold on my face. Thrain leaned in to wipe a hand over my cheeks, then lifted me in his arms and carried me over to the front yard where Cass waited. From her expression I knew she could at least guess what we had just discovered.

"Seems like someone found her before us," she said.

Thrain smirked. "Maybe he knew where to find her all along."

"What are you saying?" Cass asked.

He peered at me and raised his brows meaningfully. "Still think Aidan's mansion isn't the most secure place right now?"

Cass hesitated. "What about Hell?"

Hell? Did she really say that? I opened my mouth to protest but Thrain beat me to it. "Dallas's attack should've taught you that's one of the most obvious places our enemies would come looking."

I pressed my cheek against his strong chest, inhaling his manly scent. "I'd love to spend some more time in Scotland, if you come too."

Thrain's hot breath left a tingling sensation on my temple where his lips barely touched my skin. I thought he whispered something that sounded like, "I'd love to." But I wasn't sure because a moment later darkness enveloped me and I lost consciousness yet again.

Chapter 12

I woke up in a bed, feeling completely dehydrated. The dry sensation in my mouth made me cough once or twice before I pried my eyes open. A groan escaped my throat as I tried to push up on my elbows. My blurry gaze focused on the people around me. And lots of them. Where did they all come from?

"You're seeing double, mate," Cass said from the window. Next to her, Amber was leaning against the wall. Aidan and Clare weren't around. I scanned the room with its flowery wallpaper and antique furniture. If it wasn't for a jacket draped over the back of a chair and lots of magazines and toiletry items cluttering the surface of the dresser, I could've sworn I was in a hotel room.

"Stop reading my mind." My voice sounded raspy. I tried to clear my throat only to start coughing again. Thrain sat down next to me and raised a glass of water to my lips. I gulped it all down and leaned back against my satin pillow, only now realizing someone had covered me with a thin blanket. I looked down. Thankfully, I still wore my clothes.

I felt so plain and weak compared to the others who seemed to take the whole situation so much better than I was. Hopefully, my powers would be making their grand entrance soon because inferior wasn't the kind of adjective I wanted to use to describe me. "What happened?"

"You fainted," Thrain said, brushing a stray strand of hair out of my face. My breath caught in my throat as our eyes met. My attraction to him drew me in again, pulling me close and refusing to let me go. For a moment, we just stared at each other, lost for words. I felt so comfortable around him, and yet I wanted to run away. I had never been so drawn to someone. It was bizarre, as though we had met before and were connected or something. Like on cue, the air around us started to shimmer like tiny, faint stars on a clouded sky. I stared in awe, wondering whether the others could see it as well, or whether my imagination was playing a trick on me.

"It's the bond you share with him," Cass said.

"They share a—" Amber asked. Her voice betrayed surprise, as if it was a big deal.

"Let her rest," Thrain interrupted her sharply. I glanced at their cryptic expressions. It was obvious they tried to keep something from me. Maybe they thought I knew nothing about their world. But I did.

The strong attraction between Thrain and me wasn't natural, and certainly not something I had ever experienced before. A bond. It sounded strange, and yet it made sense. At Madame Estevaz's house, I had felt his emotions. Since I wasn't particularly perceptive and Thrain couldn't read my mind, it could only be the result of our connection—our bond.

"You must be starved." Cass winked and pulled Amber behind her. "Thrain will bring you something to eat, and then you can get some rest. Or not." I watched them close the door behind them, aware that Thrain and I were alone. Suddenly, the large room seemed too small. He cleared his throat and turned to face me. I opened my mouth to speak but no sound came out.

"When this is over I'd love to see you again," he said. I nodded stupidly. There were like a million things I could've said, clever things, something that could've made me seem more attractive in his eyes, and yet my mind remained blank.

Thrain inched closer. I watched his fingers move across the sheet toward my hand, stopping an inch away. The poor guy was probably waiting for a sign from me. The knowledge was there, and still my mind couldn't come up with anything. I kept staring at him. A soft smile crossed his lips. "Okay. I'll bring you dinner."

He stood and hesitated. I sensed he had something to say but couldn't bring himself to do it. My fingers touched his skin gently, and I marveled at how smooth his skin felt. "You know I said I had a boyfriend?" A frown crossed his dark brows. I smiled. "It was never anything serious."

"Right." He nodded, grinning, then left. I buried myself into the soft bedding and pressed my hands against my burning cheeks. Gosh, the guy was gorgeous! Granted, demons had never really ranked high on my dating list but there was something about him that made me forget what he was. Besides, I didn't need to marry the guy. With my music career about to take off, commitment would only hinder me. I smiled at the air as my mind conjured up his image. White teeth gleaming as he shot me that easygoing grin of his. Strong arms scooping me up in his arms and pressing me against his strong chest. I remembered the unbuttoned shirt at the airport and the tattoo slithering down his entire chest and wondered whether it'd seem desperate if I asked to see it. Being shy wasn't usually my thing, but I didn't want to come across as cheap, so I decided it was for the best not to mention that I knew about it.

A few minutes later, Thrain returned carrying a tray with a ham and cheese sandwich, and a cup of luke-warm tea. He placed it on the bedside table and pointed at the sandwich. "Sorry, there was nothing else in the fridge. I don't think anyone here's ever going shopping, what with them being vampires."

"It's fine, don't worry. I'm not usually spoiled for choice." I eyed the white bread hungrily, waiting for him to leave again, but he didn't seem to harbor that thought.

"Mind if I stay?"

I peered at him surprised, not sure that I really wanted him to watch me eat. "Sure."

"Great." He slumped down on the other side of the bed, leaving a bit of distance between us, for which I was grateful. As much as I fancied him, pushy guys always put me off. I grabbed my sandwich and started chewing, paying attention to doing it slow and graceful. The cheese tasted old but it was still edible. In fact, hungry as I was, I thought it was the most amazing meal I had lately.

"You know what really bugs me?" Thrain continued without waiting for my answer. "I think you know way more than you let on."

"What makes you say that?" I asked.

He crossed his arms over his chest and turned his gaze to the ceiling as though the answer might just magically appear. "I've spent my whole life among humans and know they're usually more careful and distrusting than you. You strike me as—" He waved his hand about, searching for the right word.

"Accepting?" Smiling, I took another bite of my sandwich.

"I was thinking more in the line of reckless."

"That's my middle name. How did you guess?"

Propping up on his elbow, he rolled on his side, grinning. A glint appeared in his green gaze. His long lashes threw moving shadows across his cheeks. I bit my lip as I took in the soft contour of his mouth, wishing he would kiss me. Then I realized, kissing wasn't an option when I knew nothing about him. "Do you have a surname?" I asked.

"We don't have one. But when I mingle with humans I tend to call myself Thrain Harnett."

I stared at him, mesmerized. "My name's Sofia Romanov."

He nodded, amused. "I know that, Sofia. I also know that you were born in Moscow on the first of May and that you turned nineteen last spring. You have the most amazing voice I have ever heard, but you want to go to drama school before making it big."

Gee, the guy knew a lot about me. I wondered how he had found out. "Stalking much?" The thought should've scared me, but it didn't. Coming from him, I found it flattering. It meant he was interested.

He laughed. "Just once or twice."

"You were at my last gig." I sat up, the sandwich forgotten. I remembered the guy with the hood covering most of his face. He had been there for an instant, and then disappeared right before my eyes. I had no idea how he had done it, but he was good, I had to give him that.

"I loved *Harried*. Maybe you'll sing it for me one day."

"Maybe." I looked away shyly. I was glad I didn't see him in the crowd because I might have ended up forgetting my lyrics. "Why didn't you talk to me?"

"I—" His hand inched closer until our fingers touched. A tiny spark flew between us. He laughed but didn't pull back. "Did you see that?" I nodded, ready to insist he give me an answer. "Okay, why didn't I? I don't know."

My brows shot up. "You don't know?"

"I didn't think this would ever go beyond being just a job. And then I heard you sing and I forgot everything else." His fingers closed around mine. The warm fuzzy feeling in my stomach grew stronger. I felt strangely lightheaded but tried to maintain my cool. He continued, "Your voice impeded all sense of reasoning. Cass was—busy, and I figured I'd find you later. But you left for Brazil. Once there, I couldn't pick up your trail."

"I wonder why."

"I'm thinking magic. Something concealed your presence, until it broke."

My thoughts wandered back to the hotel room. "Maybe something inside the room."

He shook his head. "No. It was on you, otherwise I could've tracked you once you left the room."

"Like something to carry around?"

"Maybe jewelry?" Thrain asked.

My mind started to put two and two together. Realization dawned on me. He gave me a silver pendant recently, but I didn't bring it with me. And the clothes I wore were my own. Except for the scarf. Gael specifically asked—no, *demanded*—that I keep it on at all times. I had found it strange, but it was a gift. I had trusted him.

"You know what I'm talking about," Thrain whispered, inching closer.

I shook my head. Gael? Of all the people in the world, it couldn't be Gael. Was it really the scarf? Something broke inside of me, and a cold sensation crept up my chest. "Just a coincidence," I muttered. "It has to be a coincidence." I knew I was fooling myself because my mind was telling me one thing, and my heart another. It was clear my heart wasn't willing to believe it when Gael had been the one to take care of me all those months.

Gael and I had known each other for a while. We had been friends ever since I visited my father to spend Christmas with him and his family in New York. Theo and I had been ice-skating in Central Park when Gael and his brother, Derrick, bumped into us. We had a great day and decided to meet again. And we did, almost every day for the entire vacation, until Theo died. While I wasn't in love with him, I trusted him and knew he would never betray that trust. Most of all, I felt safe with him. He never treated me badly, he always tried to help me and make me feel better about myself and my music. He was always there for me. I could hear my heart screaming, protesting, becoming hysterical. It couldn't be Gael. Maybe he was just a victim. For all I knew he could have received the scarf from someone else who claimed it'd keep me safe. Knowing Gael, he fell right into that trap because he cared so much about my wellbeing.

I brushed a hand over my face as I listened to my mind's arguments. Why did he take me to see a fortuneteller? Why had he been so irritated recently? I turned to Thrain. "Do you think I could make a call?" He shook his head. "A text?" I winced at the thought of breaking up with Gael via SMS. He deserved better than that.

"Not happening. It could be traced. But you can send an email if you want to."

"That can be traced as well," I said.

"Luckily, I know a thing or two about computers." He jumped up and reached down to help me. The way his hand wrapped around my fingers felt natural as though it had always belonged there. Barefoot, I let him lead me downstairs to an old-fashioned library with huge black couches and bookshelves leading up to the ceiling. Cass, Aidan and Amber were gathered around a fireplace where flames leapt at two logs. Their conversation stopped the moment we entered and all eyes turned on us.

"I think I'm having a déjà vu, only now I'm not the mortal feeling completely out of place. Funny how life can turn out," Amber said. Under the harsh light, I caught a glimpse of tiny lines around her eyes, something I hadn't noticed about the others, and for the first time the thought that she might've been mortal once entered my mind.

"We need to use the computer," Thrain said.

140

"Is it safe?" Aidan asked.

"I'll make it safe," Thrain replied. His grim expression betrayed his willingness to challenge anyone who dared defy his wishes. I squeezed his hand, only now realizing he was still holding me tight. I wondered what the others would make of it.

Amber shrugged and pointed at a notebook on the table in front of her. It was already switched on. "Help yourself. Just don't mess this up." She stood and left the room with a smiling Aidan following suit. Cass trailed behind but not before shooting us a doubtful look.

Thrain started typing on the sleek, black device. I peered over his shoulder as he closed the last browser window and caught the title 'Voodoo and South American practices of black magic'. Black magic—that didn't sound like something I ever wanted to try.

"Ready," Thrain said, pushing the notebook toward me. "You can send your email from here. Do not navigate away from his site. I'll wait outside."

I shook my head. "No, don't. I want you here. Just turn away."

"As you wish." He turned his back on me, so I began typing. By the time I finished the paragraph my back was slick with sweat. For some reason, I felt as though I had just sealed my fate forever and signed over my soul. Whatever flicker of hope I had felt inside me was now gone, blown out like a candle. I didn't even know what I had been hoping for, only that once I pressed the send button, it would be gone.

141

My index finger hovering over the key, I took a deep breath and pressed it. When it was done, I turned to Thrain with a smile, feeling guilty but not enough to stop myself from placing a soft kiss on his cheek.

He raised his hand to touch the spot. "What was that for?"

"Just so." I shrugged and got up, eager to return to the solitude of my room. I had defied my mother's wishes of marrying a rich guy. I had done the exact opposite of what everyone expected of me. How could I possibly tell him that for the first time in months I felt free? Lost but free. And it was so worth it because I was ready for something new. I was ready for *him* because I was about to fall in love—with a demon.

Chapter 13

Thrain

The way Sofia's hips swayed, she almost looked as though she was dancing her way out of the library. She looked so sexy in her tight jeans, I had a hard time keeping my gaze focused above her waist. I hoped her sudden change in mood could be attributed to my presence and the fact that she had just placed a kiss on my cheek, but my teenage-like hope was laughable. At my age, I was way past receiving kisses on the cheek from my love interests. Usually, they moved a lot faster than that, and yet I appreciated the fact that Sofia wasn't throwing herself at me the way others did. It made the whole experience more interesting.

A few minutes after Sofia left, the others returned. Cass's gaze fell on me and stayed there. The question mark on her face wasn't exactly discreet. I raised my brows. "What?"

"You share a bond with her."

It wasn't a question but a statement, and it didn't even take me by surprise. I had been interested in women before, but not to the extent of just wanting to be near her, smell her, touch her hand, and hold her near for the rest of our lives. "How would you know?"

"We're not stupid." Amber slumped down next to me and waved a hand in my face. "All this staring at each other and not being able to stay away even though your job's done, I've seen it before." With Aidan. If anyone knew what *the bond* felt like, it was Aidan and Amber. I shot him a quizzical look only to receive a very meaningful grin and a slap on my shoulder.

"Congratulations. You've just won a ticket to lifelong manipulation and headaches," Aidan said. Amber's eyes shot daggers as she slapped the back of his head. He rubbed it, grinning. "What? It's true. If that girl's only half as feisty as you are—"

"Don't even think about saying it, or you'll be spending the night in a nice place called garden. I've heard that bench's really comfortable." Amber turned toward me, her temper mellowing down a little.

"I don't know what sort of game you're playing but Sofia needs to keep a clear head. So, back off," Cass said.

"Who said *I'm* the one pursuing *her*?"

"Come on. I might be way younger than you, but I'm not stupid." She rolled her eyes. The childish

144

action gave her an innocent flair, but the dark rims were already there, signaling she'd have to leave very soon.

"Trust me, Cass. Stupid is the last word I'd use to describe you."

Her freckled face lit up, and for a moment she seemed to be the same carefree girl I had learned to love like a sister. But an instant later, the frown lines across her usually smooth forehead returned and I knew she was about to lose it again. The short temper wasn't her fault. The reaper inside her was demanding death, causing her body to suffer immense pain until she gave in.

Time to change the subject. I shot Aidan an imploring look. He clicked his tongue. I inclined my head and pointed at Cass.

"Sleeping Beauty's been gone forever," Amber said, following my line of vision.

"It's called being a vampire. It's not Clare's fault she has to rest during the day. You'd be sleeping too if it weren't for *me* helping this lot steal that Shadow book," Cass said through gritted teeth. "Come to think of it, that wasn't my brightest idea, was it? That darn book got us all in trouble. Without it, Dallas would still be alive." She started marching up and down, her hands wringing in front of her. Pearls of sweat had gathered on her brows.

I groaned and slumped deeper into the couch. The curse was taking its toll on her. Soon the reaping periods would grow longer and longer, with very little

145

time being her true fallen angel nature in between. One day she wouldn't turn back, and then she'd be lost to us forever. The knowledge had been lingering at the back of my mind ever since she turned the very first time, but seeing her like this, an empty and angry shell of her usual bubbly self, made me doubt the success of this mission.

"It's time to go," Cass said. Her voice came so low I thought she was about to faint like Sofia. I jumped up to catch her before she hit the floor, but she pushed me back, sending me tumbling against the wall. Aidan held out his hand to help me up. I grabbed it and let him pull me up.

"I'm sorry. I didn't mean to," Cass muttered.

"Don't be," I whispered. She shot me a pained look the moment she disappeared.

"She'll be gone for a long time," Amber said. I nodded, unwilling to elaborate on her unspoken question. "The period's are getting longer, aren't they?" She let out a sigh and turned toward the window, as though speaking to herself. "You know I wasn't keen on the idea of her dating my brother. And when I heard about them wanting to get married, I thought she must have a reason for wanting to tie the knot after knowing him for only a few days."

Aidan walked over and grabbed her in a tight hug. "Don't, Amber. You're only torturing yourself."

She shook her head. "Please, let me finish. I need to say this."

"You don't owe anyone an explanation." I sat down on the couch, far away from her so she wouldn't catch the expression on my face. Truth be told, I hadn't been keen on the idea of Cass getting hitched either, and particularly not to a mortal. I had thought it was just a game she played, just a wicked plan to get her out of Hell and the future her father had envisioned for her. Now I knew I had been wrong. Whatever Dallas and Cass shared, it was the real deal. Apparently, Amber had finally come to realize it too.

"I owe it to myself," Amber said.

My vision blurred and for a moment I thought I saw Sofia's half-naked shape tossing and turning in bed. She had pushed the blanket aside. Her nightshirt had rode up her long, pale legs. I swallowed hard as I tried to hold on to the image before my eyes. Sofia jumping out of bed. She was wearing an oversized shirt that I assumed belonged to Clare who was the tallest of them. I half expected her to slip out of it and change into the clothes she'd been wearing all day but instead she squeezed into a knitted, black sweater that reached down to her knees, wrapping a cord around her waist, and padded barefoot out the door. The vision broke. I blinked several times, unsure whether I had actually seen Sofia or imagined here. An instant later, the door opened and she walked in, silent like a ghost, her feet barely making any sound on the rug. I stared at her attire, my gaze settled on her shapely legs that peered from beneath the black sweater. She shot me a timid smile as she sat down next to me, tucking her legs under her and pulling the knitwear over her knees.

"We're all blaming ourselves for what happened, but do you really think things would've taken a different turn if you were more accepting of their relationship?" Aidan asked.

Amber didn't seem to notice Sofia as she tore herself away from Aidan's embrace. Her gaze focused on the woods outside the window and she shook her head lightly. "Maybe, but that's not the point. You don't understand. She was here for me when I stumbled into this world and I repaid her by judging her for who she is. I thought she was just bored and Dallas was her toy, which made me angry. This whole connection thing—I went through it. I almost died for it. I should've understood how little saying she had in choosing her mate. It happened to be my brother. So what? I should've understood. Now he's dead."

"Do you think that's a coincidence?" I asked.

"What?" Her attention snapped to me.

"That one always dies."

She shrugged. "How would I know? We have two examples. That's not exactly years of research data."

"I'll come back later," Sofia mouthed next to me. I shook my head, signaling her to stay. My own guilt flared up as Amber continued.

"I think he knew she was lying to him and yet he stayed. If I supported them maybe he'll still be alive, and she wouldn't have turned into this thing that gorges on suffering and death. I was so preoccupied with my own self-pity, I didn't see how hard I was making it for everyone else."

Sofia rubbed her hand over her face. I could sense how uncomfortable she was, so I leaned over to squeeze her hand.

"Sorry you had to hear my rant. It wasn't my intention to ruin your day." Smiling apologetically, Amber walked out the door with Aidan following her. I turned to Sofia slowly, my own apology already lingering on my lips.

"She's gone through a lot," I said.

Sofia nodded. "The bond she described, is that what we have?"

Her question took me by surprise. I dwelled on it for a moment until it occurred to me that, even though I had been born into this world, Sofia was the one with the knowledge. She was the incarnation of a very powerful soul, a soul that might just hold the key to her own destiny and wisdom.

"I can sense you when you're not here," Sofia continued slowly. "I felt your emotions, and I can somehow feel your touch even though we haven't—"

"Me too." Meeting her gaze, I inched closer and wrapped my arms around her. My nostrils picked up her scent: a mixture of lavender, honey and something much sweeter. I inhaled deeply until it reached my very core. When I looked up again, her expression was soft, dreamy. "There's only one way to find out." I pushed my index finger under her chin and lowered my lips onto hers, savoring her taste slowly at first, then with more vigor. She reminded me of gingerbread and sweet wine, of grapes ripened under the Tuscany sun. My hand wandered around her neck to draw her closer to me until I could feel her chest crushed against mine. Her heartbeat raced as fast as mine, they were beating almost in tune. The air crackled around us, charged with electricity. She parted her lips, as though to welcome more. But this was all I wanted to take from her—for now.

With hesitation, I peeled her away from me and pressed my forehead against hers. "I've been wanting to do this ever since I saw you at that club in NY."

Her laughter sounded more like a moan. "You did?"

My finger traced the contour of her chin, down her throat to the collarbone hidden underneath her sweater. "I think we have the answer to your question. Maybe Amber's right and the danger that seemed to come with their connection was just a coincidence, but I'm not taking chances." I lifted her chin until our eyes locked. "From now on, you're staying beside me at all times."

"I'd rather trust your instinct than mine because, as it seems, last time mine let me down big time." Smiling, she raised her lips to mine and I grabbed them in a sweet kiss, more than happy to oblige.

Chapter 14

Soul mates are said to be two souls destined to be together, programmed to recognize each other across time and space. I didn't know whether that was the truth, but I was inclined to believe it. I wasn't naïve to assume just because Thrain and I were attracted to one another, everything would always turn out well, but I would give it a chance in spite of our differences in character and background. Where I came from fate played a more important role than choice. We didn't believe in choice, only in that what's meant for you will reach you in time, and if you embrace it with your arms wide open it might just stay with you forever and bless you with more happiness than you could ever envision.

Thrain was fate. I knew it. I had recognized it during our kiss. When our lips locked, a floating sensation washed over me, like I was diving in sparkling blue water with the soft rays of light caressing my skin. And then the tingling began like a tiny spark between us. That tiny spark became a silver thread shimmering in a million shades as it wrapped around us and drew us closer. In that instant I knew I had found the one to complete me. But I also knew Thrain's fear was justified. The others had been oblivious to it, but I could feel the darkness around that bond, feeding from it, trying to draw us into a direction that would decide over our future. I doubted I could change that direction, but I vowed to myself I would rethink every step twice before making a decision.

I snuggled against him and let my thoughts draw me in. Thrain must've misinterpreted my sudden silence though because he leaned back and pulled me closer, mumbling something like, "We can take it slowly if you want."

"I'd like that." The steady beat of his heart and the silence of the night drew me to a place of love and comfort. Eventually, I closed my eyes and gave in to the need to sleep, and for the first time in weeks that unnerving darkness didn't descend upon me.

***

I didn't know how long I had been sleeping when the noise of cawing woke me up. I sat up groggily and squinted against the unnatural brightness of the ceiling light, wishing I could tell whoever was causing

152

this much noise to shut up and let me catch some more snooze. My hair caught in something. "Ouch," I yelled out.

"Stand still," Thrain said. I stopped stirring as I watched him from the corner of my eye as he unwrapped a strand of hair from around the button of his shirt, then smiled. "Sorry."

"Thanks." I got up and peered out the window at the darkness stretching over the woods and mountains in the distance. My gaze searched the unnerving bird and found it perched on the windowsill. It was staring at Thrain as though unsure whether to trust his intentions.

"That bird's been watching me for hours," Thrain said, coming up behind me and grabbing me in a tight hug. My hands brushed his naked arms, soaking up the warmth of his skin. Not for the first time I wondered whether his unnatural heat was a demon thing.

"It's been following me for weeks," I said.

"A stalking bird?" Thrain laughed softly. "Now that's the kind of stalking I like."

My heart almost stopped at the thought of him with another woman. "Been stalked by many?"

"I was just kidding."

"Right." I nodded, feeling silly for my sudden outburst of jealousy. It wasn't like me. I wasn't usually the possessive type.

"What do you think it wants?" Thrain asked.

153

I shrugged. "My first guess was to warn me, but I'm not so sure now. It seems to know me."

"Maybe you should talk to it."

Admittedly, that thought didn't cross my mind. Talking to demons and vampires and what else not was one thing, but to a *bird*? I smirked. Wasn't happening. Once I started communicating with a crow, I knew my sanity was probably going down the gutter. Maybe one day I'd pluck up the courage and make a fool of myself, but not yet. There were more pressing issues to take care of.

"Is Cass back?" I asked. "She owes me a one-on-one."

"She's in the living room," Thrain said, so I got up, prepared to leave. He grabbed my hand and pulled me down on his lap, his hot breath brushing my cheek. "Hey, haven't you forgotten something?"

A kiss. Grinning, I gave in wholeheartedly, then pulled out of his embrace and left, wishing there would be many more to come. Soon but not soon enough.

Cass was already waiting for me in the living room. The others were gathered around her, Amber sitting on one side, Clare on the other. Aidan stood by the window, his gaze scanning the darkness. He was expecting someone or something. I would've liked to ask but I bit my tongue to keep quiet. Prying wasn't attractive—it was one of the few virtues my mother had tried to teach me. Unfortunately, this one was the hardest to follow because it completely defied my personality.

"Look who's decided to join us?" In spite of the glow on her face, Cass seemed bothered.

I sat down on the couch farthest from her. "Any news?"

"Me?" She shook her head, her red mane brushed the collar of her baggy top that accompanied her baggy jeans. "Nope, mate. You?"

"Don't think so." I knew she was talking about my smooching with Thrain and I wondered what gave me away. My gaze moved to Clare—tall and blonde, just like me before I dyed my hair, but with a mysterious elegance I would never possess. Next to her and funky Cass, Amber almost looked normal. But only almost.

"Do you have any idea how old he is?" Cass asked.

"Not old." Maybe a few hundred years, thousands tops, but most certainly beyond his mid-creepies. The thought didn't scare me because physical existence comes with a shelf life, but not our soul. I had lived before dying and being reborn. Thrain had just never died.

Cass clicked her tongue. "You might harbor a different opinion about the 'not old' part if you knew the truth. He could basically be your—" She gestured about with her hand. I noticed her nails were bitten to the point of bleeding. "Anyway, I can't believe you two are dating now. I'm gone an hour and you're already making out."

"We didn't make out," I said indignantly. We didn't, did we? It was just a kiss. Though a hot one that would soon lead to more but, as things stood, we hadn't done anything naughty yet.

"Stop wasting time, Cass," Aidan said from the window. "Whatever they do is none of our business. We need to work on our plan, find out how to unleash Sofia's powers so she can finally return Dallas's soul to his body. Which reminds me—" he turned to face me. A glint appeared in his intense blue gaze "—I believe there's something Cass and you wanted to talk about. Mind if we stay?"

I shook my head. The guy was so friendly and civil, how could I kick him out of his own house? Besides, I figured since Amber had been the one to convey the message during that TV show and she was dating him, he probably knew just as much as she did. He was the one I needed on my side. "I wanted to talk about my sister, Theo. You said you knew where she was and that, if I helped you guys, you would let me see her."

"Uh-huh." Cass regarded me coolly.

"I want to know what happened." I raised my brows at her.

Cass inhaled sharply and I knew I had to prepare myself for bad news. "Theo's in Hell because she killed someone." I opened my mouth to protest, but she raised her finger to stop me. "She killed Gael's brother, Derrick. I don't know why she did it, but apparently she was in danger and he killed her, which doesn't make any sense. If she killed him, how could he kill her, unless they killed each other at the same time?"

"Cass," Aidan hissed. "Get on with it."

"That's the problem with vampires, they're always so grumpy." She rolled her eyes at me. "When Aidan killed his crazy ex, Rebecca—"

"She wasn't my ex. She turned me," Aidan interrupted.

Cass continued unfazed. "We didn't know we'd end up with a crazy killer in Hell. Distros is the home of our supernatural visitors, but it's also the only unsupervised dimension." I nodded, confused, wondering where she was going with this. Cass moistened her lips. "Before Rebecca died, she put a spell on a very important book to take it with her into the Otherworld. I don't think she knew what to expect on the other side, but she probably hoped she'd get her chance to escape when others came looking for the book. And she did, with this lot's help." Cass pointed at Amber who smirked at her. "Amber descended into the Otherworld to retrieve the book. I took it back home with me for safekeeping, but that didn't turn out so well. Rebecca killed Dallas and fed on Theo's life force. She must've targeted your sister. We suspect she did it with the intention to find out who you are."

"Life force? How is that possible when she's already dead?" I asked. The thought of my sister's death almost choked me. Clare pushed a glass of water across the table. I thanked her, then turned my attention back to Cass. My trembling hands clasped the glass tight until I feared it might just break.

"Blood is the essence that keeps the physical shell alive. Life force is the essence of the soul. Without blood, a mortal dies. Without life force, a soul may forever be extinguished," Cass explained.

"Is Theo—" My voice broke. *Forever gone*—I couldn't speak out the words.

"Her soul's alive," Cass said. "The gate keepers saved her, but when life force flows from one person to another, so do the person's memories." She leaned forward, her green eyes focusing on me, her voice dripping with meaning. For the first time, I was awestruck. Although the others had already pointed out that Cass wasn't your usual immortal being, I didn't really consider the magnitude of their implication. But now, staring into her striking eyes and listening to all the knowledge she shared with us, I understood why the others looked up to her even though she was the youngest. Cass was the one who had access to the dead, both to the mortal and the supernatural souls. She had seen Heaven and Hell.

"Hey, Soph, are you listening?" Cass asked, jolting me out of my thoughts. "It's not just Rebecca we're talking about. Others will come for you so we need to work on a plan to unleash your powers and protect you at the same time because the stronger you get, the more you'll be in danger."

I still didn't understand. "But what would she want from me?"

"To bring her back from the dead," Aidan whispered.

I took another sip of my water. My mind raced a million miles an hour. There were so many unanswered questions I had no idea where to start. I opened my mouth to ask how a vampire, strong enough to cause complete havoc in Hell, depended on someone like me when a faint memory hit me. It was more of a blur, no pictures, not strong enough to make complete sense of it, and yet I knew I had something important here. "I can only return a soul into a body. If there's no body, there's no way to keep the soul in the physical realm."

Aidan shot me a questioning look. "And you know that *how?*"

"Past life regression. She seems to have a lot of that in her dreams," Thrain said from the door. My head turned sharply. I hadn't heard him come in. How long had he been standing there, listening? He smiled and inched closer, slumping down next to me. His arm wandered around my shoulders naturally as though it belonged there. As though we had been dating for months. For a moment I froze because I didn't know how the others would react. What would they think of me, hooking up with a guy I barely knew? Thrain pulled me closer and I gave in because no one's opinion mattered.

"I don't see anything in my dreams."

"You have the wrong impression of regression," Thrain said. "Everyone expects it to be like watching a movie in front of your eyes, but in reality the actual focus should be on some of your senses. You need to pay attention to smell, taste and your body's responses rather than to what you see and how you feel because pictures and emotions can be deceiving. The actual memories consisting of bits and pieces will always come later. The darkness you see in your dreams is something from your past life, maybe a last thought that's supposed to convey a message. I think that's what keeps triggering the regression."

A message. Just like the crow. I had figured that much and yet I had no idea what I was supposed to understand. Time to talk to the bird then. I sighed and nodded. "Makes sense."

"But we still don't know how to tap into those powers of hers," Cass said. "I wish we had someone to ask."

"Have you tried *Google*?" Clare winked at me.

"Of course we have, mate," Cass said, grinning. "That was my first choice." I couldn't tell whether she meant it.

"Wanna go to bed? You must be tired," Thrain leaned in to whisper in my ear. I didn't fail to register the double meaning. Waiting for my answer, he raised his brows, his expression betraying amusement. I lowered my gaze, lest the others notice my scorching cheeks. Damn, what was it with this guy and me putting words in his mouth? "Of course I wouldn't mind joining you, but I'd rather you got some sleep," Thrain continued.

There it was again—that innuendo I kept hearing. Did he mean I wouldn't get any sleep if he stayed with me? I groaned inwardly at myself and my brain's inability to stop overanalyzing everything he said.

"I need to get some fresh air," I said, getting up. Maybe the night air would clear my mind and help me gain a new perspective.

"Don't let her stray away from the house," Aidan said to Thrain, already assuming Thrain would be playing babysitter.

I frowned. "Actually, I need to be alone."

"Five minutes," Aidan said.

"Control freak," Cass muttered.

He shot her an irritated look. "Need I remind you Dallas's life depends on—"

Tuning out, I got up and headed for the back garden, leaving the others behind. It wasn't so much the fresh air I needed but the solitude to do the one thing I should've done already. And for that embarrassing display of human stupidity I didn't need witnesses.

Chapter 15

The Scottish air smelled clean and crisp, like after a brief summer shower, but without the earthy scent of soaked wood. I closed the backdoor behind me and hastened my pace to the nearest tree in the distance—a gnarled old thing stretching proudly against the black canvass of the night, battered from years of changing seasons and stormy weather, but not yet beaten. Millions of stars dotted the sky above. The moon built a perfect crescent over my head, its light illuminating the paved path beneath my feet as I left the safety of Aidan's mansion behind me.

As expected, the crow sat perched on a low hanging tree branch, already waiting for me. I felt silly leaning against the thick trunk, my gaze fixing the unnaturally large bird, my fingers fidgeting with the hem of my sweater. Even though it was summer, a freezing breeze crept up my naked legs and my skin turned into goose bumps. I crossed my arms over my chest to keep warm.

Gosh, I had never felt so stupid in my entire life. I took a deep breath to steady the sudden onset of nervousness. Surely I had done harder things than talking to a bird and yet I didn't seem able to utter a word. Eventually, after a few long minutes of staring at each other, I said, "Hi."

The crow's head bobbed to the side, beak opening as though to speak back to me.

"You've been following me around a lot." The bird flapped its wings. I smiled, getting into it, even though I still felt silly. "Why don't you just spit out what you're trying to tell me?"

The crow's loud caw sliced through the silence like a knife, startling me. My heart jumped in my throat as it flew over my head and landed at my feet. I kneeled down and held out my palm, unsure what to expect. Another caw, and the bird inched closer. Its feathers, black as coal, seemed to soak up the light around us. The shiny eyes shimmered like dark puddles in the moonlight. I gazed into them. Something was there—dark and menacing and foreboding. Lurking beneath the surface of my perception was the answer I had waited for, and yet I couldn't grasp its meaning.

"You want something," I whispered. The crow cawed and spread its wings. "Whatever it is, you'll have to queue up like everyone else because it seems everyone wants something from me."

The crow let out a shrill, piercing sound. The earth began to quake. I had to grab on to the tree to support myself. In horror, I watched something pitch-black, darker than the night, enveloping the bird. It looked like thick smoke swaying in the wind, inching closer toward me. Uneasiness settled in the pit of my stomach. I knew I should turn around but couldn't. Literally. My legs were frozen to the spot. I willed them to move, but my feet wouldn't obey my brain's command.

A murmur filled the air, like hundreds of voices that merged into one, making it impossible to tell whether they were male or female. And then the flapping of wings started, louder than ever before, reminded me of a morbid melody. Something wasn't right. I tried to scream, but no sound escaped my throat. When I finally came to my senses and realized what was happening, it was too late. The earth cracked just an inch or two, but the fissure grew in length and width until it built a large gap that reached as far as I could see back to the house. The crow swooped over my head and flew headfirst down into the gap.

Still unable to move, I frowned as I peered into the impenetrable darkness at my feet. Time seemed to stand still. Even the wind had stopped. The only noise came from my labored breathing. And then the earth began to shake again and the air around me changed from the fresh-smelling scent of trees and leaves to the scent of disease and decaying bodies. I held my breath as I kept staring down. I feared something would creep out, and yet my curiosity wouldn't release her hold on me and kept me glued to the spot. I wanted to know what was down there. My heart hammered like a drum in my ears. In spite of the cold, beads of sweat covered my body and trickled down my back in thin rivulets that soaked my clothes.

Something was heading for me. I stared ahead but couldn't see a thing, and yet I could tell it rose from the depth of the earth with unnatural speed, heading straight for me.

Run! Run now! A voice yelled in my head. The flapping of wings grew louder and more ominous. A cold sensation hit my face. The wind had started to blow again, but it was coming from the wrong direction. It blew in from below me, carrying that scent of disease and decay, blood and—burned flesh. My stomach clenched in response. A yelp escaped my throat as I stumbled backward, my back hitting the tree trunk. Grazing my palms on the coarse bark, I steadied myself and then tore through the trees as fast as my muscles would let me.

The sinister presence followed close behind me. My head jerked back every few seconds, my gaze searching the night even though I knew I wouldn't be able to discern darkness from darkness. And dark they were, both the night and the creature. As I kept running through the bushes, twigs snapped under my feet and scratched my legs. I winced at the searing pain in my thighs and the burning sensation in my lungs.

Something touched my back. I screamed and turned, kicking and punching against the warm shield.

Strong arms enveloped me and drew me close, forcing my wrists to keep still. Through the haze in my mind and the fear gripping me, I made out Thrain's voice, "Shush. I'm here, sweetheart. Now, breathe." He began to rock me softly as he cradled my head against his chest. The steady beat of his heart calmed me a little.

I peered up into his green gaze, shining unnaturally bright in the night. "I saw it." My words sounded muffled and indiscernible.

"It's okay. Everything's all right. You're safe with me. Come on, breathe with me." His palms started to rub my back, up and down, soothing me. My body relaxed but the shaking didn't go away. "Come on, breathe with me. In and out."

My chest rose and fell as I tried to get a grip on my nerves. The heat from his body warmed me in the chilly breeze.

"Better now?" Thrain whispered. I nodded and looked over his shoulder. The strange, fog-like darkness was gone now.

"Thrain? Did you see it?" I searched his gaze.

He shook his head. "No. Tell me what you saw."

I could feel my body stiffening again as though fighting the memory in my head. "I tried to talk to the bird when the earth cracked and something rose from below."

"A demon?" His voice betrayed surprise, disbelief.

"Maybe," I said softly. Looking up, I noticed his smile was gone. I moistened my lips as I tried to make sense of the array of thoughts and pictures in my head.

"That doesn't make any sense. What would a demon want?"

Why was it so hard to believe? I didn't usually care what others made of me, but Thrain's opinion mattered, even though I knew it shouldn't. If *he* didn't believe me who would? "Maybe he wants the same thing as everyone else," I finally added, hoping Thrain would catch the drift.

He lifted me up in his arms in one fluent motion. I wrapped my arms around his neck, holding tight but keeping a bit of a distance between us. "Let's go back to the house and we'll talk there. If what you say is true, you're not safe out here." He didn't wait for my approval, just took off through the night, moving like a sprinter aiming for gold. I realized I must've been running for a long time because I couldn't see the house. We moved so fast the woods became a blur, yet he didn't even seem to break a sweat. Eventually we reached the house but he only put me down inside the kitchen, then went about pouring me a glass of water, instructing me to finish before recalling the event. I did as he said, still miffed at the idea he might not believe me.

"I got you something to eat." He pointed at the tray across the oak table and sat down on one of the chairs, motioning me to sit next to him. I lifted the lid to peer at a variety of sandwiches. I was hungry but didn't take him up on the offer. Even though my tiny breakfast barely covered a day worth of meals, eating was the last thing on my mind.

"I'm a bit tired. I think I'll eat upstairs." Even though a sandwich barely covered a day worth of food, eating was the last thing on my mind. I wanted to be alone with my thoughts to analyze what just happened. But Thrain didn't seem keen on the idea.

"No, Sofia. This is something the others need to know now." He grabbed the tray with one hand and squeezed the other under my elbow, forcing me up. I struggled in his grip but gave up as I realized if a guy could sprint through the woods carrying my weight, I was wasting my time and effort resisting his wishes.

I sighed and let him lead me to the library. I wasn't even surprised to find everyone was still there, still sitting on the same spot as before, still staring at us when we dropped down on the couch and Thrain placed the tray in front of me, his gaze urging me to eat. I shrugged and started chewing on a sandwich. It was so silent, the sound of my cutlery and plate reverberated from the walls. My chewing reminded me of a siren they could probably hear in China. My stomach grumbled in agreement as I shoveled down the food, ignoring the unnerving calm. A few bites in, Cass broke the silence and the questioning began.

What had I seen? What had I been doing before seeing it? What did I make of it? To that question I had no answer, but Thrain seemed to have made up his mind already.

"A demon chasing her—" He ran his fingers through his hair, lingering at the back of his head as though to massage a tensed spot.

"It *is* strange," Cass agreed. The soft skin around her eyes had visibly darkened, giving her a gaunt expression.

I finished my meal and wiped my mouth with a napkin, then pushed the tray aside. Clare jumped up and mouthed something that sounded like she'd be right back. I watched her grab the tray, which made me feel instantly guilty. I barely knew her and yet I could already see the dynamics here. She did most of the work while the others sat around. Even though she was the most striking one out of the bunch, she was also the one that seemed to blend in with the furniture. There was something depressing about her, something that made me want to burst out in tears whenever I looked at her. It wasn't a nice way to feel about anyone and yet I couldn't help myself. By the time she returned a minute or two later, I had already forgotten about her, which strengthened my opinion that, as stunning as she was, something grave had happened to her that had robbed her of any passion.

"Rebecca had help," Aidan said.

Cass nodded. "From the Shadows. We know that already."

169

"No." He shook his head. "They were only after the book, but Rebecca was after Theo."

"But Theo and Rebecca were in Distros long before you and Amber showed up. Why didn't she just attack Theo at the first opportunity when you weren't there? It would've been a lot less complicated."

"I think she didn't know who Theo was—until someone told her," Aidan said. "After our arrival, I guarded the perimeter, meaning she had no chance to get anywhere near Theo."

I peered from one to the other, soaking up all the details. But my confusion persisted. "Who are the Shadows?" The moment I asked, I knew the answer already. Shaman warriors with eerie black eyes. Dark magic. Astral travel. And then a pact. I shook my head, begging my mind to glue the pieces of the puzzle together. But they remained seemingly unrelated flashes in my head.

"A group of immortals we've been fighting for centuries," Aidan explained grimly.

"They astral traveled to Hell and put a spell on the whole dimension so no one would hear my cries for help, or Dallas's for that matter," Cass said. From the frown on her face I could tell they weren't exactly her friends.

"Are they involved?" Clare asked.

I nodded. "They were involved a long time ago."

Four pairs of eyes shifted toward me. "You know them?" Aidan asked.

"I think I did once." I pressed my fingers to my temples to catch another glimpse of the pictures in my head, but the memories didn't return.

"What are odds, huh?" Amber said, regarding me. For the first time, I noticed something in her eyes. Respect. Awe. Like she hadn't really taken me seriously until now. I found myself smiling confidently, even though confidence was the last thing I felt inside. Amber continued, "How did you meet them?"

Void. I shook my head.

"Do you just happen to know about their existence, or did you actually get to talk to them?" she persisted.

I shook my head again. "Can't remember."

Thrain wrapped his arm around me and pulled me closer. I leaned against him, thankful for his support. I dropped my gaze, then looked at the carpet awkwardly, noticing two tiny red stains. Spilled wine that could be weeks, months or even years old. The silence was an awkward one.

Eventually, Cass resumed the conversation. "Gosh, this is sort of getting us nowhere. Our suspects so far are a crazy vampire—" she held up a finger "—a group of morons that wouldn't know friendship if it bit them in their ass—" she held up another finger, then a third "—and, last but not least, Thrain's suggestion of a demon, which about covers all of Hell. Throw in a few succubi and we're only looking for the entire paranormal world."

"You've got a point," Thrain said. "As long as we don't have any other clues, everyone's a suspect. Let me show Sofia to bed and then we can talk some more."

Cass winked. "Make sure it's to bed, not *into* bed."

Heat scorched my cheeks, and not for the first time. I was slowly starting to look like a huge shrimp. "Are you sure I'm not missing anything? I'm not really that tired." Actually, I was because I hadn't slept in a long time, what with all the travelling and time differences.

"We'll be all right. Get some sleep. You might not get it again any time soon," Cass said.

I smiled and said goodnight even though I knew I was probably the only one who would go to bed. Thrain accompanied me up the stairs to the bedroom I had been assigned. In the hall, I found myself standing in front of the door with him holding my hand as he gazed down into my eyes. We stared at each other in silence, my face still flushed though I doubted he could see it in the soft glow of a night lamp. It seemed we had both lost the ability to talk; either that or the silence suited us more than the pressure of speaking meaningless words that wouldn't make a difference in who we were and what our purpose was on Earth. We belonged together. It wasn't so much a discovery as a fact. I didn't need to tell him. I knew and felt in my heart that he was thinking the same.

"Sofia." His warm breath caressed my skin as he inched closer and wrapped his arms around me. I let him draw me to his chest and pressed my head against his shoulder, my fingers drawing slow circles on his arms. His mouth covered my neck in soft kisses that sent shivers down my spine.

"We should make a deal." I smiled at his raised eyebrows. "I want you to tell me something about you every time we kiss. This way we can at least follow the usual protocol of getting to know each other before jumping in with both feet."

"Sounds like a good deal, but only if you promise to do the same." His lips lowered onto mine. I parted my lips for him and melted into his arms. His intoxicating scent hit my nostrils, making me dizzy. A soft moan escaped my throat, but instead of making me feel silly for giving in so quickly, he broke off our embrace and took a step back. His heated gaze settled on me as he ran a hand through his hair.

"What?" I asked, self-consciously.

"You're hot."

"Is that what you like about me?" I loved the compliment, but guys always wanted me because of my looks. Usually, it was either my blonde hair or my long legs. I wanted Thrain to be different. I wanted him to be attracted to my inner being, not to something that would fade over time.

His big hands cupped my face, forcing me to look at him. I hoped my eyes didn't betray the hope inside me. "I don't like you because you're hot or because we share a bond. I like you because you're smart and tough. You have values that are rare in our times, like being responsible way beyond your years and wanting to achieve something in life."

"Thank you," I whispered.

"You said you wanted to know more about me." I nodded sensing a big revelation that wasn't easy for him. Thrain took a deep breath and continued, "I've been a nomad for centuries. I don't think I've ever settled down in one place for longer than a few months—until I met you. When this is over I want to be near you, wherever you are. And if you don't want me, then I'll wait in the shadows until I've conquered your heart and you find me worthy of your love."

He was already conquering it. I had never felt closer to anyone in my entire life, as though we were one and the same being. "I'd like that very much."

I, too, would wait for him because I wanted to be with him. I wanted to fall asleep and wake up in his arms. He kissed my mouth softly. I parted my lips to grant him access. His soft lips sent shivers down my spine. He pulled away softly. "Now, it's your turn." His eyes met mine. His encouraging grin urged me to look inside myself and find something I wanted to share with him, something that would help him feel as close to me as I felt to him.

I cleared my throat, considering my words. "As a child I used to daydream of getting lost in the woods and being found by a dark stranger. I remember the way I pictured his eyes: green with brown speckles, surrounded by black lashes that would give him a mysterious look."

He laughed out loud. "I hope it's me. It would mean your first prediction came true. I want to know everything about you."

I let my childhood memories flood my mind as I traveled back in time. "My father left my mother for a woman he met on a rare visit to the city to stock up on provisions. Her name was Marie and she was an actress filming a movie. When she returned home, he left with her and I didn't see him for years. I hated him for what he did to me and my mom for a long time."

"Is that why you find it so hard to open your heart to anyone?"

His question took me by surprise. I laughed uncomfortably. The need to negate his statement flared up. I decided against it because, thinking of it, he had a point. I didn't want to fall in love with a guy, settle down and start a family. The trip to Brazil with Gael was about the only plan I had made with a man, and that wasn't even a plan because he had surprised me with the flight tickets. Guilt grabbed hold of me. Gael. I had liked him but was never in love with him. He was already forgotten, as though he never existed. I hadn't even checked my emails to read his response.

"It's okay," Thrain said, misinterpreting my silence. His fingers rested on my lips as though in order to keep me silent. "We'll take it slowly. We don't need to make any plans if you don't want to. Will you be okay alone in your room?" I nodded. He placed a soft kiss on the tip of my nose. "If you need me I'll be downstairs. Sleep well."

"Thanks." I watched him stroll down the stairs carrying his head high. His pace was confident the way only a guy, who knew he was everything a girl could ever desire, would carry himself.

Chapter 16

Thrain's scent and taste lingered in my mind as I jumped under the shower to wash off the traces of a long day. My skin seemed to tingle where the hot water hit it. My whole being felt as though I was floating in the vast universe with nothing but him to anchor me. If it weren't for the cold air sending shivers up my spine to remind me of time and space as I stepped out of the shower, I would've continued to float in that dreamy state. I let out a delighted sigh and went about brushing my teeth with the visitor toothbrush, then put on a nightshirt and jumped under the covers. It wasn't like me to feel so at home in a strange place and yet, in this house among these people, I felt as though I had returned to a place where I belonged. That instant I knew I could never restore my old life. I could never go back to the old me. Sure, the music career would have to continue because it gave my life meaning and I had a mission to fulfill, but I knew the lost and scared Sofia from before was gone.

With the soft covers wrapped around me, I fell into a deep yet uneasy sleep and while the darkness I had grown to fear didn't return, I knew something was watching me, waiting for me to make a mistake. I wondered what that mistake was.

Morning had yet to break when I woke up with a jolt. The moon lay hidden behind a thick veil of dark clouds. The room had noticeable cooled down. I shivered and closed my eyes again, ready to get back to sleep. But there was a soft, indiscernible whisper, which must've been what woke me up in the first place. I slipped into my jeans and the sweater Clare had borrowed me, and pushed the curtains aside.

Gloomy shadows still covered the woods. I opened the window to let in the freezing night air and strained to listen to determine where the whisper came from. My lungs burned from the cold as I inhaled deeply, held the breath, then exhaled. Only then did I notice the small writing on the glass, the same word I saw at the hotel in Rio: HELP. Someone needed me.

Branches snapped below the window. Something caught my attention in the distance. I peered at what looked like a white curtain. It took me a while to realize it was the long hair of a girl, framing a pale face. My heart almost stopped beating and a whimper escaped my throat.

"Theo." The word choked me, brought me on the verge of tears. Leaving the window open, I stormed out of the room and down the stairs, through the kitchen into the back garden. She wasn't there, but I recognized the spot where she had been standing. Near the gnarled tree with its low-hanging branches that almost brushed the lush grass beneath.

"Theo," I whispered again, trying to be still so I wouldn't wake up the others. My naked feet sank into the damp grass as I picked up in speed, my eyes scanning the area frantically for a glimpse of that almost white hair that was so typical of my family. And then I saw her twenty feet away. She was staring at me, her eyes looking sad. She put a finger to her lips, as if hushing me to be quiet. In slow motion, she gestured a no, as though I shouldn't seek her, and then turned her back on me and took off again. Panic rose inside of me. I wanted to see her. She needed my help. I could feel it.

"Theo, wait!" My voice was raspy, already hoarse from the cold. I sprinted through the trees, determined to catch her, and only stopped when a crow flew over my head and perched down on a branch a few feet away from me. I leaned against a tree to catch my breath.

The clouds broke and the moon come through, casting an eerie light over the place and the big crow— the same one that turned into a dark entity and chased me. I felt my heart racing, my palms sweating as the bird cawed.

179

Think, my mind screamed. *Think*. I remembered the word HELP appearing out of nowhere. At that time, when I opened the window in Rio, I also spied the crow instead of my sister. My stomach protested. My ears began to ring at the mere thought, but what other explanation was there? The crow was warning me before something happened.

It was a trap.

I could see the mansion in the distance, its contours stretching menacingly into the night. The people in there were my friends, the crow wasn't. Or was it the other way round? So far I didn't have any proof that they were really on my side. Cass had yet to keep her word and grant me access to my sister. What if Gael indeed was trying to protect me from something? Maybe he was trying to protect me from the immortals in there.

The craw cawed. I took in the beautiful, black feathers and dark eyes. Something—like black fog—lifted off my mind, clearing my thoughts. What was wrong with me? That mansion was my safe fortress. I had to run back, but would I make it?

My muscles started to work hard as I traced the way I had come through the trees, heading for the safety of the mansion's wall in the distance. For a moment, I thought I picked up the sound of a child's voice calling my name. Was I abandoning my sister who needed me in her hour of need? I clenched my teeth and ran faster when something hit my back and I stumbled forward, twisting my ankle in the process. I scrambled a few feet away, then turned slowly and noticed he was still standing in the same spot.

With dread filling my heart, I looked into the one face I had been dreaming of my whole life, always forgetting upon waking up, only to remember later. It was one and the same reoccurring dream of an old woman and the pact she had signed. His face was more beautiful than I remembered it, his voice sounded as smooth as dripping honey, dark and melodious, and so very deadly. His dark eyes stared me down. They remind me of the dark puddles I avoided at night as a child in the fear I would fall into them and never get out.

"Shadow," I whispered to myself.

"I'm impressed that after so many centuries you still remember me." He inched closer and reached out. I stared at his outstretched hand but didn't take it, noticing the sheath bound around his hip, hiding a sword. I almost expected him to lunge at me and pull me up, maybe even drag me away kicking and screaming. But he didn't. His hand hovered a few inches away from me, brushing through the air as though to touch an invisible wall. A frown crossed his beautiful features, all pale skin smooth as marble and shiny, black eyes. His hair had changed from shoulder-length to a more contemporary cut, still black but with blonde spikes. It suited him, made him more ordinary looking, which was a dangerous combination because it made me feel as though I could outsmart him. But no one outsmarted a Shadow—and surely not Devon.

"What do you want from me?" My attempt at infusing confidence into my voice failed.

Devon smiled but it didn't quite reach his eyes.

"Do you want to kill me? Is that what you came for?" I continued.

"No blade of mine could kill you, Sofia," he said. "Or should I call you Esmeralda?"

The name rang true. That's how I had been called and yet I felt it didn't suit me anymore. I was the same soul, but my life had shaped me into a different person. Or maybe it was my mate's existence that made me strive to be someone else. I scrambled to my feet when a sharp pain pierced my swollen ankle. I winced inwardly and hoped the emotion wouldn't show on my face. "What are you here for?"

He kept staring, his black eyes irritating the hell out of me. Eventually, he reached beneath his cape and pulled out a shiny object dangling from a long chain, then tossed it toward me. I caught it in mid-air and twirled it around my fingers as I peered at the tiny moonstone carved in the form of a butterfly.

"Wear it," he said.

I cocked a brow. "Why?"

"Because it'll protect you."

"Who said I need protection?"

"Trust me, you'll do soon." His face remained unreadable, as though he wasn't even capable of feeling emotion.

My insides turned hot and cold. "What do you see?"

"That I can't tell you because it is not I who sees but our Queen. Deidre is the Seer. Don't you remember, Esmeralda?"

He was using my previous name deliberately, maybe to mock me, maybe to trigger the trust I had once felt toward me. I remembered him, but the trust I had once felt toward him was long gone now. "Queen Deidre."

More memories flooded my mind. I saw she had been beautiful, the only Shadow with black eyes and snow-white hair, which defied the Shadows' nature of black hair and black eyes that shined like liquid oil. I only glimpsed her once in her true form, many years before my fate befell me, but not long before she was turned into something abhorrent—a soul transferred into the body of a dying girl, trapped forever between life and death as she fed on her own people's life force. Upon hearing of her fate, I had felt sorry for her. Until she betrayed me. Instead of granting me a few more years to live and the chance to be reborn in exchange for my powers, she left me dying at the hands of the reaper who had been watching me for weeks, maybe even longer. In my hour of suffering, I despised both her and myself for trusting her people.

"You still haven't answered my question." I took a deep breath and pronounced every word slowly, as though speaking to a child. "What do you want from me?"

183

My tone displeased him for his eyes narrowed. He was used to being shown more respect, which I wasn't willing to give him. He had pulled a stunt on me centuries ago; if he ever wanted my trust again he would have to earn it.

"It's not a matter of what I want," he said softly. I groaned. The guy deserved a metal for his ability to talk in circles. "Come with me and we'll protect you from the evil that's after you." His gaze remained focused on me, intent to read my expression, as he reached out but didn't touch me. He was too composed, too forthcoming, as though he wanted me to believe he was giving me a choice. For a moment, I looked away to give him the impression I was actually considering his offer when all I could think of was ways to get the hell away from those eerie eyes.

"Still, what's in it for you?"

He sighed. "We see it as our duty to protect the weak and helpless."

Despite being mortal, weak was not a word I'd ever use to describe myself. I was a fighter who didn't take life for granted. How could he see me as weak? Fury boiled inside me. I raised my chin a notch to meet the surprised glint in his gaze. "I'd rather die than come with you." As my pulse quickened, the confusion in my mind began to lift. Why didn't he inch closer when I was at his mercy? The answer dawned on me quickly. Magic. I knew nothing about the vampires that lived in this house, or their abilities. But maybe teleporting wasn't the only thing they were capable of.

Both Aidan and Amber didn't seem to feed on blood, and they both didn't shun the sun. They must've placed an invisible shield to form a perimeter around the property so no uninvited guest would cross it.

The knowledge gave me enough courage to take off through the trees toward the mansion rising against the morning sky. It wasn't so much 'taking off', more like limping at the pace of a snail. I dared a look back to see the Shadow staring after me. His face was a mask of surprise and anger. The air beneath him stirred and a girl appeared, her blonde hair swaying in the breeze giving the impression of a huge halo floating around her. She took a step forward and patted the air with pale hands as though to touch an invisible wall.

A ghost had no body and would just walk through such a barrier, which meant the girl was a Shadow, just like Devon. They had tried to deceive me yet again, and I almost fell for it because the moonlight had made it easy to mistake her face for my sister's.

My ankle throbbed but I only stopped when I reached the back door leading to the kitchen. Wincing, I leaned against the cold wall and pressed my palms against my knees as I watched the dark figure in the distance and the girl, barely more than a white blur, standing next to him.

I knew better than to test my new theory, and yet the questions burning on my tongue needed immediate answers. The sun hadn't risen yet but I could already see the moon disappearing behind the hills in streaks of gold and orange and copper. In the moonset, droplets of morning dew covered the grass and leaves. I buried my fingers into a nearby bush and then touched my face. The moisture invigorated me and soothed my cracked lips as I headed back for Devon, eager to find out whether I was right.

My legs moved swiftly, the pain in my ankle forgotten. As I approached, the girl moved away from me, a few steps at a time, as though she didn't want me to get too close to her. I stopped a few feet away from Devon, making sure I wasn't crossing the barrier that had protected me before.

"You came back." He smiled. It looked just as fake as before, plastered on his beautiful lips to lure me in and give me a false sense of trust and safety. I didn't fall for it.

"How do I unleash my powers?"

He cocked a brow. "You don't know?"

"If I knew I wouldn't be asking."

"You don't need to unleash them, Sofia. They're already there, waiting to be put to the test."

His answer took me by surprise and for a moment I just stared at him, searching his features for a giveaway that he was lying. "How do I use them then?"

"Come with me and we'll show you." He reached out again, his fingers pressed against the invisible shield.

I shook my head. "First answer, then I'll consider your offer."

"No. You need us more than we need you."

186

"What makes you say that?"

"Don't you want to be with your sister again?" He pointed behind him at the small figure peering at me from between the trees. Her hair swayed in a breeze I didn't feel, her white, baggy gown made her look frail and sick. I could make out the details on the hem and around her thin wrists, and yet I couldn't really see her face through the blur that seemed to envelop her.

I swallowed down the lump in my throat. "My sister's dead. The only way I could ever be with her is if I joined her in the afterlife."

"That's not true, and you know it," he said. "We could help you find a body and teach you to raise her."

I considered his words. Ever since Theo died I had wanted to know what happened to her. For a long time, I would've given anything to turn back the time so my baby sister wouldn't go out that fateful night in search of me. If I hadn't insisted on playing the gig and took a taxi like every human being in New York, she wouldn't have needed to leave the house. If I didn't tell her how much that gig meant to me, Theo would still be alive. I desperately wanted her to live, but raising the dead? It seemed so...wrong. So scary. Would I be creating the same person as before, or a dead copy of her former self? A zombie. I needed to know how to use my powers and what those powers entailed before making a decision.

"Just tell me how to use them," I said.

"Your voice is your most powerful weapon, but be careful what you speak for it might just come true."

I nodded, thankful for the advice. "What else?"

"Blood is the carrier of your powers, but it can't be any blood. Use it to ground yourself and for everything else that you wish to achieve."

My mind went wild. Pictures of an old woman dipping herbs into a puddle of blood and spreading it around her in a circle moved in front of my open eyes. I could see her shifting back and forth as though to soothe a crying child, but what she held in her arms wasn't a child. It was the lifeless carcass of an animal, something furry like a weasel, but I couldn't be sure because the head was cut off.

Bile rose in my throat. I bent forward and retched. I threw up a few times, nothing but bile. When I rose to my feet again, the pictures in my head were still there, but I felt better.

"You have strong memories," Devon said. I nodded and he continued, "Don't fight them because they're the key to your future." I cleared my throat to get rid of the scratchy sensation, ready to speak. He held up a hand to cut me off. "I'm a Shaman, not what you are, so that's about all I can teach you. However, we have others who know about your kind, and they will be happy to assist you. Come with me, Sofia."

Many years ago I would've joined him gladly. I couldn't now. "I'm staying."

"You need help if you want to gain control of your powers. The vampires in there can't help you. We can."

I shook my head defiantly. Two tiny lines formed around his mouth, but if my answer didn't please him he didn't say so.

"Don't you want to help your sister?" His tone became softer. Even though I could sense his bluff, my heart skipped a beat.

"She needs my help?"

He nodded. "She needs to leave that dreadful place. I see her in my dreams. She cries for you. She knows it's your fault, but she won't blame you if you help her return."

My anger flared. Theo's death was my fault, but he had no right to say it. It was a trick. No matter what hardship Theo might endure, deep in my heart I knew my baby sister would never think badly of me. Without a word I turned on my heel and walked back to the house. His gaze followed me, I felt it burning on my back long after I entered the kitchen to prepare myself breakfast. I wasn't hungry, but I knew I would soon need my entire strength for what lay before me.

Chapter 17

For a house full of immortals, it remained surprisingly quiet for another hour, which suited me just fine because I needed time to think. I regretted brushing Devon off, but only until I remembered he had betrayed me once. He would probably do it again if the opportunity presented itself. I didn't know what motivated me to trust the Shadows in the first place all those years ago, but I vowed to search my memories and find out. In the meantime, I would keep away from them.

I stirred two teaspoons of sugar into my tea and took a sip, burning my tongue in the process. Assuming I could tap into my past life and make sense of all my memories, what then? Could I even stomach using blood in my rituals without fainting or throwing up every two minutes? Devon had said I should use my voice. Even if I figured out in what way, would I be able to find the right words?

Sighing, I took another sip and turned to the window. The sun stood high on the horizon now; its light cast a glowing hue on the green grass and blooming flowers. Birds chirped in the distance, calling to their mates. My connection with Thrain should've kicked in this morning when I left the house to run after a faceless apparition. Either Thrain was a sound sleeper, or he hadn't spent the night here. For a moment, jealousy gripped my heart and darkened my already bad mood. I had enough on my mind already without the guy adding to it by making me all obsessive where he had been.

I didn't hear him come in until he stood behind me and placed a kiss on the back of my head. "Good morning. Slept well?" His hand brushed my hair.

I turned to face him. My heart skipped a beat as I peered into his spectacular eyes where the sun seemed to break into hundreds of different shades of green. My fingers moved of their own accord, tracing his jawline and running down his throat to the undone button of his shirt. I peered at the tan skin peeking from beneath and the black outline of his tattoo.

"Do you want to see it?" Thrain asked, breathless. I nodded and he started unfastening one button at a time, his gaze still settled on me. Heat rushed to my cheeks, but I couldn't take my eyes off his sculpted chest. "What do you think?"

About his muscles or the tattoo? I nodded appreciatively and let my finger trail down the contours of a green dragon wrapped around an eagle, it's beak open as though to bite off the dragon 's head. "It's a symbol of something, isn't it?"

"It stands for the endless battle of two forces, none of which is entirely good or entirely bad."

"Is that what you think of your origin?"

"Not entirely. The battle's supposed to represent my own nature. Like Cass, I don't exist to serve one plane only." Taking a deep breath, he smiled. "If you really want to know what I think of my origin, I'll tell you. It's the most beautiful place in the entire world, above and beyond. But I also think it's cruel to have known it and then be cast out, even if only for a while. I have a purpose to fulfill on Earth and in Hell before I can return to my origin, but the knowledge doesn't make being cast out any easier to bear."

"I thought your origin was Hell?" I asked, confused.

Thrain laughed softly, his eyes burning with excitement. "No, you got that part wrong. I might be a demon, but that doesn't mean I was born in Hell. Angels and demons are created in the City of Tiebetran, which is a dimension far away from Hell. Maybe one day when I'm allowed to get back, I will show you where I'm really from."

I swept my hands through his hair. It felt like spun silk between my fingers. I could sense sadness in him.

"I'm sorry. I hope you'll be able to return soon." I realized my palm was pressed against the eagle's head now. With regret, I peeled off my fingers and placed a gentle kiss on his lips.

"Don't be. Everything in life suits a purpose." He cleared his throat but didn't button up his shirt. I'd rather he did because his half naked body was triggering all sorts of naughty thoughts.

"Where were you last night?" I blurted out before I could stop myself.

"Work." His fingers moved beneath my chin, forcing me to face him. "There's no else, Sofia. I wouldn't leave you if I didn't have to." I nodded, relieved, so he continued. "I've found out a few things I'd like to talk to you about, but we need to wait for the others. If I'm right, you're in great danger."

Didn't I hear that one before? I smirked and opened my mouth to tell him nothing scared me when the door burst open and Amber walked in. Her gaze moved from Thrain to me then back to Thrain, and she frowned. I thought Thrain would at least have the decency to cover up, but his nakedness didn't seem to bother him as he sat down on a chair and pulled me on his lap. His hands moved around my waist, lingering on my body as though they had always belonged there.

"Aidan says they were here. He can smell them. Did you allow her to meet with our enemies?" She opened the backdoor and left it open, sniffing the air. A breeze carrying the scent of flowers and damp earth carried over.

"Meet who?" Thrain asked, brows furrowed. I could see his confusion on his face and felt bad for not telling him straight away what happened at night. I didn't want him to think I kept secrets from him.

Truth was, I had been so preoccupied with my own abilities that I hadn't even bothered to find out what the others could do. Of course, if a safe perimeter had been cast around the house, chances were high the owner might have a way or two to find out.

"Shadows," Amber said. Any hope of her not busting me pulverized into dust. I took a deep breath, ready to explain, but she beat me to it. "I think they lured her out, and trust me, they're kinda good at it. She saw them and ran away, which is the only reason why she's sitting here with us this instant, rather than locked up in a labyrinth mountain. The breathtaking view wasn't so bad, but I wasn't so keen on a life-long sentence in a freezing room and lots of weird talk from some freaky kid that wouldn't look out of place in *The Exorcist*."

"You know Deidre?" I bit my lip, realizing I had just spilled out the one secret I wanted to keep to myself—at least for the time being.

She nodded, her gaze staring at me so intently I feared she might just be able to peer into my soul. "I do. In fact, I owe her the pleasure of near death, almost being lost in the otherworld forever and, of course, raising Rebecca who, if you don't remember, is the one who killed my brother. Now, what did

Deidre want? Another mortal pet with a paranormal ability to add to her trophy wall?"

She wasn't particularly keen on the Shadows, was she? Why wasn't I surprised? "I only saw Devon. He offered to protect me and teach me how to use my powers."

I felt Thrain stiffen. Amber snorted. "Heard that one before. Whatever they offer, reading the fine print is always worth it 'cause their deals usually suck. Look who's decided to join us." She turned her head to the door a moment before it opened again and in walked Cass followed by Aidan.

"You know that Devon guy's slowly starting to piss me off," Cass said to Thrain. "I should've got rid of him a long time ago." He nodded and I wondered whether she meant it literally as in kill him or something. My eyes widened. She just shrugged and slumped into a chair opposite from me. I thought she'd care to elaborate but she just kept staring at Thrain who stared back at her. Apart from a frown or two, their faces remained expressionless, but that was enough to tell me they had some mind thing going on. Maybe coming from the same place, Heaven and Hell, made them able to communicate with each other.

"How did you know they were here?" I asked Aidan.

"They can't touch gold. I have infused it with magic and set up a safe perimeter around the house and the property."

195

I nodded because the latter part I had figured out myself. Nothing new there. He still had to answer my question. "Yes, but *how* did you know they were here?"

"Keep your friends close and your enemies closer. The vampires and Shadows have been entangled in a war for such a long time, he can smell them. Literally," Amber explained.

Aidan shook his head. "It's not just that. The shield works like an energy field. They know about the shield but decided to touch it anyway. I think Devon wanted us to know he was here. Maybe they're after her—" he pointed at me "—but they might not be the bad guys in this particular instance."

"Would you team up with them?" I asked.

"When Hell freezes over." Cass jumped up, knocking the chair over in the process, and took off through the backdoor.

"Cass, wait!" I watched Thrain go after her, probably to calm her.

"She was friends with them once," Aidan whispered.

Amber nodded. "Needless to say, being friends with them is like letting the wolf in sheep's clothing near the flock."

"So sorry about Cass's temper. She can be a bit intense," Aidan said.

I nodded. "Figured that much. If I were to turn into a reaper every few hours, I'd probably take it much worse than she does."

"It's not just the reaper thing," Amber said softly. "She can't live without her mate. Literally. If he dies, bad things will happen to her."

I felt compelled to ask what those things were, but social etiquette told me to shut up and let it be. It wasn't my business. If Cass wanted to tell me, she would've done so already. "The more reason to get this over and done with." I was eager to reveal my big secret, ready to give my powers a try, but not because I wanted to. The air was thickening and too many people were already on my tail. Time to keep my word and then think of a way to get out of this forever, preferably with Thrain by my side.

"Can you really communicate with the dead?" I asked Amber.

Her brows shot up. "How do you know?"

"I remember you from the show. You were introduced as a necromancer."

"Yeah, that's what I am. Sort of." She moistened her lips, hesitating. "Let's just say, I'm still learning. And it's a long learning process." Aidan threw her an amused look like they had some sort of private joke going on.

"What is it like? I mean talking to the dead."

"Ask her when she's actually given it a try," Aidan said, grabbing her in a hug. From the way she slapped his arm, then perched a kiss on his lips, I could tell they felt comfortable around one another, as though they had dated for ages. And yet Cass had told me they only met a few weeks ago. A pang of jealousy hit me at how loved up they seemed. I wished I'd experience that sort of intimacy one day, that feeling of love and total devotion to someone. Sighing, I turned away to give them a bit of privacy. A moment later, Aidan cleared his throat and resumed the conversation. "I always figured a mortal would have more questions. Amber certainly did when she was—"

"When I wasn't a bloodsucker, albeit one that's on a diet thanks to a lovely spell," she finished for him, tapping a finger on her thigh. "I wonder what'd happen if the ritual were ever reversed."

"You can't reverse a ritual," Aidan said. She narrowed her gaze, ready to argue with him again. I feared I might not get another chance so I decided to return the topic of conversation back to me.

"Actually, I have tons of questions. I just didn't want to sound rude."

"Spill," Amber said, turning away from Aidan and crossing her arms over her chest.

"You said the vampires and Shadows have been enemies for centuries. I know how strong they are, but I haven't seen much from you yet. What can you do apart from teleporting to places?" I bit my lip, avoiding their gazes, unsure whether I had crossed the line. For someone, who tried to avoid sounding rude, the way I had just put my question sounded anything but respectful. "I'm sorry, I didn't mean to sound like you don't have any other abilities," I heard myself say, making it worse.

"It's okay." Aidan walked over and patted my arm lightly, his gaze searching Amber's as though to ensure she wasn't going to have a fit. "We have superhuman strength, speed and hearing. And when we feed on someone else's blood, we absorb a life's worth of memories. None of their secrets will remain hidden from us. Not even future ones. We're basically connected with them, meaning we can influence their thoughts."

I nodded, impressed. Then a thought hit me. "So, if you were to drink my blood all my secrets would be revealed to you, and you could turn me into a brainless zombie who follows your every command?"

"All your secrets, knowledge, memories. Everything. We couldn't turn you into a zombie, but you'd have a hard time defying our wishes." He didn't get my hint. Or maybe he did. If he tasted my blood, he could sort through my memories, which in turn meant he could look through my past life and tell me how to use my powers.

"I no longer drink blood, Sofia," Aidan said, sensing my thoughts. "Please don't ask any of us because a tiny drop from the source could turn us into raging maniacs."

I shook my head. "I wouldn't. But is that why the Shadows fear you so much?"

Amber blinked. "It is, isn't it? I always wondered. You know what really sucks? Being a vampire and having to figure everything out as I go along."

"Might be time to open up some sort of support club," Aidan said. His smile told me he was joking but his eyes remained dead serious. Come to think of it, that wasn't such a bad idea. Maybe they could do the same thing for voodoo priestesses.

"I want to use my powers," I whispered the same moment the door burst open and Thrain walked in with Cass trailing behind. She raised her eyebrows at me so I repeated the statement, this time a little louder even though I had no doubt she could understand me just fine.

"When?" Thrain asked.

"Today. Now."

He regarded me for a long second, his eyes staring me down, questioning the sanity of the idea. "You don't know how to use them."

I nodded. "That's true, but I doubt anyone could ever teach me. Voodoo is an ability, a calling." Don't ask me where I knew that part from. Wisdom just seemed to pour out of me, as though something had happened that kept triggering my memories. I smiled, self-satisfied, for a moment feeling like the important one in this room, not the usual odd one out because I wasn't immortal or as special as the others. I had an ability they didn't possess.

Thrain opened his mouth to speak when Cass nudged him in the ribs, her gaze throwing daggers. "She's the expert, mate. She knows what she's doing. What do you need, Sofia? We can get hold of anything you want."

200

I swallowed the sudden lump in my throat and tried hard to avoid Thrain's disapproving look. He was worried and I couldn't blame him. My mind searched through my vague memories for indicators of what I might need for my ritual. "Herbs—dried lavender and myrrh to banish bad spirits."

"Amber might be able to help out with that part, if she's not running away first," Aidan said.

"Or worse—fainting." Amber snuggled into his arms. "Sorry, can't help you. The last ghost I raised tried to claw my eyes out."

Cass rolled her eyes. "Don't flatter yourself. You didn't raise her. In fact, you didn't even realize she was a ghost until I told you."

"Whatever," Amber mumbled.

I shot Thrain an amused look. He didn't retaliate. Well, if he didn't want to play along, then he'd have to stay out of my affairs because there was no turning back now. "I'll need blood."

"You mean a drop?" Cass asked.

I hesitated. "More like a bucket."

"Shouldn't be too hard to get in a house full of vampires," Thrain muttered. "Might as well hit the blood bank now before they close, huh, Aidan?"

"I need fresh blood," I whispered. All eyes turned on me. "What?" I shrugged. "Never seen the real deal?"

"We have, but have *you*?" Aidan asked.

"Let me think what else I might need." I dropped down on the couch and turned away, ignoring his question. What could I say? That I had seen lots of blood in my visions and that even the memories of its smell made me sick to my stomach? If I told them, they wouldn't take me seriously. My confidence in my abilities was already non-existent. "Candles and white chalk, a drum and a bell. I think that's it. If I remember anything else, I'll let you know. Now, if you'll excuse me I'd like to retreat to my room while you get everything." I stood and walked to the door with the others staring at me. Reaching the doorway, I called over my shoulder, "Oh, and a blade. And something personal that belonged to Dallas, preferably something soaked in blood."

I didn't wait for their answer, just ran upstairs and locked myself inside the room, my hands shaking as I pressed my back against the closed door, letting my emotions take hold of me. What was I doing? I wasn't this confident voodoo priestess that could hold a ritual to return the soul of the deceased into a body. I needed more time. My hands rummaged inside the drawers to find some cigarettes. When I didn't find one, I slammed the drawers shut and dropped to the floor, pressing my back against the wall. It took me several minutes to calm down and convince myself I didn't need cigarettes. I went to the bathroom and dived my hands into the cold jet of water to cool my skin. Looking in the mirror, I noticed the dark circles framing my eyes. I needed rest, but I couldn't have it yet because I had a purpose to fulfill.

I wanted this. I might not be ready, but I had no time to waste. The excitement at the prospect of finding out what I really was grabbed hold of me, pushing my fears to the back of my mind, my fingers already itching to give it a try.

Chapter 18

I barely got an hour of sleep before a knock on the door jolted me out of the scary darkness that seemed to take over whenever I closed my eyes. Groggy and jetlagged from all the traveling around, I sat up and called for my visitor to come in, almost expecting Thrain to pop through the door. But it was Amber who brought me lunch, then plopped down on the bed to join me for company. I ate my lasagna and listened to her small talk, my mind half-busy with my own stuff. I still had no idea what I was getting myself into but I figured time would tell. Besides, it wasn't like I had a choice. If I truly and honestly wanted to talk to my sister, I had to figure this voodoo business out sooner rather than later.

"You still want to do this?" Amber asked as she accompanied me to the living room downstairs.

I stopped in my tracks and regarded her intently. "Isn't that what you want? To save your brother from sure death?"

"Of course." She hesitated, and in that instant I saw countless emotions on her face. Hesitation. Doubt. Hope. "I just—" she paused to take a deep breath "—please don't mess up. I don't want him turned into something he isn't, like a flesh eating, brain dead zombie." The last word barely made its way out of her mouth. I smiled at her overactive imagination.

"So you'd rather see him dead?"

Her eyes grew wide and she shook her head vehemently. "No! Never. But I'm pretty sure he would prefer that option."

I nodded and touched her arm gently. "Don't worry. I know what I'm doing." No idea where that came from because obviously I had no clue since I had never practiced voodoo before—not in this lifetime anyway. However, I was ready to give it a try. It wasn't like I actually believed anything I might be doing would actually work.

She nodded, and for the first time a real smile lit up her face. I marveled at how pretty she looked, and so very British with her chubby face and curves in all the right places. Striking in her own way.

I knew I should be wearing a robe or flowing gown for the ritual, but since I never asked for one of those, I figured my jeans would suffice. Hopefully, the gods and goddesses wouldn't see it as a lack of respect and would still listen to my plight. I accompanied Amber to the library. Gathered around the fireplace, where a hungry fire lapped greedily at dry wood, were Aidan and Cass. Thrain sat near the window, the farthest place from me.

The carpet had been removed, revealing a gleaming wooden floor. On the coffee table, pushed to the far left, were the things I had ordered together with a bottle with a red liquid. My stomach clenched instantly and I felt all color drain from my cheeks.

"Is that—" I couldn't even get the word out.

"Blood?" Cass raised her brows. "Nope. It's red wine. We thought you might need a bit of a pick me up. Guess we were right."

I felt my pulse steady again, as though a huge weight had just been lifted off my chest. "Right." I nodded and peered down at the floor, wondering where to begin. The chalk. I grabbed it from the table and drew a large circle, about a hundred and fifty inches in diameter, in the middle of the room, then lit several candles inside.

"Do they need to be of a specific color?" Amber asked. "Sorry, you didn't say, so I chose white."

"White's great." I smiled and grabbed the drum, my hand wandering over the tight skin on top, so smooth to the touch. And then the first memory came back to me. A warm summer night. People gathered around a fire and me holding a drum in my hand. A strong sense of peace washing over me as my hand started to pound, slowly at first, then faster and harder. Sweat poured down my back, the sheen layer making my clothes stick to my skin. I closed my eyes to savor the feeling. When I opened them again, I realized the drumming noise didn't take place just in my head. My hand was moving, beating a rhythm I had never heard in this life. The others were staring at me.

I smiled and put the drum aside. "Sorry. I got carried away."

"So that's how it works," Cass muttered.

"She tried her hand at magic," Aidan explained, pointing at Cass. "Didn't work out so well, huh?"

Cass shot him a venomous look, and I turned away, eager to get acquainted with my new materials. I spread the dried branches and herbs around me, then grabbed the white material someone had folded next to a dagger and took my place in the middle of the circle.

"I'll need the body," I whispered. "I can't do this if he doesn't have one."

"Dallas's body is in a safe place. I've brought you something that belonged to him," Cass said.

"Is this it?" I swallowed the sudden lump in my throat. My hand hovered over the shirt, but I didn't touch it.

Cass nodded gravely. "It's what he wore when he died."

The brownish stains on the front couldn't be mistaken for anything else. Judging from the amount of it and all the slashes and holes, it wasn't a nice death either. I peered at the dried blood for a few seconds, then peeled my gaze away because just thinking of gore and what else not wasn't doing my stomach any favors. And yet I knew I had no choice. "I need a sacrifice. More blood."

"He's my brother. I'll do it," Amber whispered.

"No. It has to come from me." Cass raised her chin defiantly, daring anyone to disagree, but Amber and Aidan remained quiet. I glanced at Thrain. He peered back at me, brows drawn, lips pressed into a grim line.

"Everybody, step into the circle, please." I raised my hands over my head to signal we were about to begin. Amber, Cass and Aidan sat down in front of me, inches away from the white line around us.

"I'm a demon," Thrain said. "I doubt anything you raise could ever hurt me. Besides, I'd rather watch from here in case I need to step in." Reading his worried expression, I could see my safety mattered to him. The realization made me feel all warm and cozy inside. I wanted to run over and kiss him for good luck, but I feared if I left the circle I might not have the courage to start over.

"Sure. Whatever you see, don't get involved," I said. Thrain nodded and with that I proceeded. Looking at the materials in front of me, I took the bell, which felt cold in my hands, and rang it twice as I began to chant, "The circle is closed." My voice started low but steady and rose in intensity as I gained confidence. "Raise this spirit and bring it home safely."

The others remained quiet. I don't know how much time passed, only that a sense of peace washed over me, and I embraced it like I would a long lost friend. The room slowly dissipated into nothingness and the faces of the others became blurred until I was no longer aware of their presence. The only thing I could hear was the drum.

For a long time, I just focused on the sound of my voice competing with the drum. And then my mind became clearer and sharper, my intentions more pronounced, and I saw the room through semi-darkness. Though I wasn't sure whether I even opened my mouth, I spoke in a language I didn't understand, begging the gods and goddesses to gather at my command and grant the gift of life for a recently deceased soul. I dropped the drum, grabbed the white shirt with one hand, wrapped it around Cass's wrist and retrieved the dagger, piercing it into her palm. She gasped as the sharp blade cut through skin and flesh, but I didn't let go. With one hand I held her wrist in place and with the other I carved a symbol I didn't recognize so deep her blood soaked the shirt and the virgin white became a tainted red. The sickening smell of iron filled the air. It didn't bother me as I put the dagger aside and resumed my drumming.

I could feel the strange presence emerging from the left side. With soft, hesitant steps it came closer and stopped at the edge of the circle. Amber let out a shriek. Aidan grabbed her in his arms and started whispering soothing words in her ear. My gaze, however, fell on Cass who just sat there and stared ahead as though she could see the entity and, unlike Amber, wasn't afraid.

"How do you—"

"I'm a reaper, mate. Seeing the dead is my business now," Cass interrupted.

I nodded and resumed my drumming, watching the young man from the corner of my mind. Confused, his eyes darted across the room, never falling on anything for longer than a second or two. His mouth hung slightly open, his neck was covered in blood, dark shadows framed his hazel eyes, but nothing could cloud his beauty that resembled Amber's so much. Not even the deathly pallor. I focused on him and imagined him in a different time, with full lips curled into a smile and the smooth skin on his neck untouched by the beast that had torn it to shreds. I imagined him full of life with his cheeks flushed and his eyes gleaming from the love he felt for his mate, Cassandra.

Something flickered in the ghost's gaze, and I knew he had just started to remember his life, his love, his dreams. "Dallas, follow my drum and it will take you to where you belong," I whispered in that strange language.

And then the drumming began again: loud, firm, making my heart pump harder. Sweat started to pour out of me, soaking my clothes. My voice rose and fell as my hands moved even faster. My own spirit left my body and started to float, then took off through the woods, flying at an unspeakable speed with the ghost following behind. All I could see were the woods below, but I could feel the exhilarating power of the wind in my hair. The cold breeze made my damp skin shiver, and yet I didn't stop until I reached a huge mansion below me. The drumbeat slowed down to let us descent through the mansion's roof into a tiny room where the body of a young man lay on a bed, covered in white sheets that made his skin look even paler. The gash on his neck exposed tendons and bones where the flesh had been ripped out. I focused on his golden hair that seemed to catch the few rays of light falling in through the drawn curtains.

"You're home, Dallas. But you need to return inside your body," I said, smiling.

The ghost hesitated, then took another step forward and reached out for his once mortal body. Slowly, his hand began to sink inside the human flesh. He leaned forward until he disappeared half inside, then completely. Dallas's body began to shake uncontrollably. From the corner of my eye, I noticed a shadow behind me. Was it his guardian? I had no time to find out because the door burst open and a man hurried in, his powerful energy frightening me. My heart began to pound hard as he stopped next to Dallas's body, then turned to face me as though he could sense my astral body.

"Thank you," he whispered, his stunning green eyes glinted. I didn't need to ask who he was. The resemblance to Cass was uncanny. I stared at him, mesmerized, until I remembered I had a job to do.

211

I nodded and fell back into the beat of the drum, rising through the air to return to the huge Scottish mansion. The way back seemed longer, filled with quiet and yet also with a sadness I didn't understand. Tiredness washed over me. The whooshing sound in my head became painful, and the light hurt my eyes. I was tempted to descend and rest in the woods below, if only for a brief moment, but I kept going. I could feel my body pulling me back. Aidan's mansion appeared in the distance when I broke down and everything went black. In the cold enveloping me I could feel someone touch my shoulder with freezing fingers.

"You must go back."

I shook my head lightly, signaling I didn't want to. Not yet. The icy fingers clamped around my shoulders and shook hard, forcing me to sit up.

"Go, now!"

Groaning, I began to ascend again and headed for the mansion. I was so tired, it took me a while to reach it. Only when I opened my eyes did I realize I must have closed them at some point. My hands rested on the drum and my head had rolled back as though in sleep. I pulled myself up, and the dizziness faded a little. My heart was still pounding hard in my chest.

I cleared my throat and straightened my back, then rang the bell to signal the end of the session.

"You've done it. Thank you so much," Cass whispered, two tears rolling down her plump cheeks. I

212

nodded and let her hug me because it was easier than to protest. The sudden weariness pressing down on my chest made me want to hide under my blanket and sleep off the fatigue that seemed to come from the core of my being. And yet I couldn't because my work wasn't done yet.

"Thrain, can I have some water?" My throat felt hoarse as I spoke, my voice sounded alien in my ears. He hurried over with a glass of water and I drank it hastily as I signaled the others that they could leave the circle. For a few seconds, they just stared at me before the questioning began. I sank into Thrain's arms as I answered dutifully, my attention focused on Cass. The long nails were gone now; the menacing flair around her had vanished. Her skin seemed to glow, her whole being radiated light and—darkness, but not in a scary way. Just different.

"Gotta go," she said.

I nodded, understanding. She had to see Dallas. If I were her, I'd want to see my mate too instead of engaging in meaningless small talk. With a last smile, she took off.

"That's enough," Thrain said and scooped me up on his arms, ignoring my protest that I wasn't finished. In few long strides, he carried me up the stairs to my room.

"Cass isn't just any angel, is she?" I whispered as he sat me down. He nodded and sat down on the bed next to me. His big hands cupped my face; his green eyes met my gaze with an expression I couldn't

213

interpret. "Thank you for helping her and for trusting us." And then he kissed me softly. I opened my mouth to say that I would do it again. Any time. I would do anything for him. But he pressed a finger against my lips, forcing me to listen. "Thank you for being here with me." I shrugged to show it wasn't a big deal. His lips grazed my earlobe, sending shivers down my spin. I let out a soft moan.

"There's something I haven't told you," Thrain whispered. "I've been waiting to meet my mate for a long time. I thought it'd never happen and that maybe I might not have one. And then I met you." He moistened his lips and ran a finger down my cheek. "You're beautiful and more amazing than I ever hoped for."

My heart skipped a beat as he whispered in my ear, "Promise you'll always stay with me. No matter what." He looked at me expectantly. A tear slipped down my cheek. In that instant, I knew I had fallen in love with him and that the bond we shared would make this love grow stronger.

"I promise," I said softly.

He smiled and leaned closer until our lips almost met. "Soph, I'll follow you everywhere. I'll do anything you want." His lips crushed mine. My mind began to spin and I let myself fall into his embrace, abandoning my own being to become a part of him, even if only for a few brief seconds. The room seemed forgotten. My fingers began to unbutton his shirt when a loud screech pierced my eardrums. I broke free and pressed my hands against my ears to stop the unnerving sound.

Chapter 19

The screech piercing my eardrums came out of nowhere. If it weren't for Thrain to jump up and run outside, I would've thought it was all happening in my head again, which wouldn't surprise me in the slightest. My palms pressed harder against my ears to drown out the noise as I followed a step behind Thrain. He turned and frowned at me.

"What?" I mouthed.

"Please, stay inside." His voice was low, barely more than a whisper. I was amazed to find I was able to hear him over the shrilling screech coming from outside.

I shook my head. "There's no way I'm staying here and you get to have all the fun." For a moment, our gazes locked in a fierce battle for control. The corners of his lips twitched, and I found myself smiling with him. He seemed to find my defiance endearing just as much as I found his protective nature one of the most attractive features about him. I grabbed his hand and dragged him behind me out the door. "Come on. You're wasting time."

He sighed but didn't argue, which suited me just fine. I had enough distractions already and didn't need another one. The noise came from the woods, near the gate. My shoe soles barely made any noise on the cobblestones as we took off down the declining path. For a moment I even felt a bit like the immortals, until my breathing started to sound like a whistle and I vowed to give up smoking. By the time Thrain and I reached the gate the noise had stopped. Aidan and Amber were already there, searching the thicket.

"Did you hear that noise?" I asked. "What was it?"

Aidan stopped in his tracks and turned to look at me. "What noise?"

I groaned inwardly. It had all been a figment of my imagination. The fact that I couldn't distinguish between fact and fiction was slowly starting to piss me off. "You didn't hear it?"

"Nope." He cocked a brow. That didn't make any sense. Why would they be running out like maniacs if they didn't hear anything? Aidan pointed behind him at the gate. "I felt their presence."

"And I picked up his thoughts," Amber said, touching the wall. "Shadows."

"I thought so too," Aidan said. "But it's different. Look—" He leaned forward to smell a stone in the

217

wall. I inched closer and took a whiff. All I could smell was rain and dust.

"I smell it too," Amber whispered. "It's strange. So similar to their scent and yet not quite. What bothers me though is the fact that it's on the inside of the wall."

I followed her line of vision from the wall to Aidan whose face had just turned into a mask of fury. "They wouldn't dare enter my property."

"Last time I checked they literally couldn't enter so maybe it's just a coincidence," Amber said.

Coincidences were nothing but poor excuses to shrug off the unbelievable, my grandmother always said. My gaze scanned the trees and bushes around us as the others decided to get back to the house and start searching the area for any intruders. But they didn't need to.

He was waiting for us in the living room, sitting on the couch like an invited guest. Lost for words, I blinked several times, unsure whether I was seeing a ghost. And yet I knew it was Gael because no ghost would ever regard me the way he did. Cold. Arrogant. Accusing. I cleared my throat, suddenly feeling guilty for dumping him via email. He didn't deserve it.

"So you're Gael, and mortal. That certainly explains how you got in," Amber said, planting herself in front of me.

I appreciated the concern but pushed her aside and took a step forward. "How did you find me?"

"There's a lovely invention called IP address, which is quite easy to track. Obviously, I took the first flight because you just disappeared and we were worried sick about you." Gael inched closer and reached out for me. I hesitated for a moment, then decided that not grabbing his hand was just rude. So I touched his skin, marveling at how cold it seemed. As though he had just stepped out of a freezer.

"I thought you knew how to avoid tracking," Amber said to Thrain.

"He does," Aidan said, his gaze still focused on Gael. "He just chose not to."

I turned to Thrain, my gaze throwing daggers. "Why would you do that?" I wished he would've told me so I could prepare myself for my ex starting to stalk me.

"You both need closure. I don't want to be the rebound." Thrain's hesitation told me he was lying. I felt there was something else he chose to keep from me. I liked him mysterious but not secretive.

I narrowed my gaze at Gael. "I'm perfectly fine. I'm sorry I didn't tell you I was going to spend some time with a few friends."

"Why did you disappear?" The accusatory tone in Gael's voice made sense, and yet there was something else I couldn't quite pinpoint, something dark and angry.

"I needed a break."

"Come on, let's give them some privacy," Amber said.

Thrain shook his head. "No." His attitude surprised me. I had fulfilled my mission of returning Dallas's soul into his body so, according to our bargain, I was free now, even though not freed from danger. Whatever the Shadows wanted from me, they were probably still after me. Thrain's concern touched me deep within my heart. I shot him a reassuring smile, then turned back to Gael.

"I'm really thankful for everything you've done for me, but you and I are over. Nothing you could possibly say will change my mind. I'll call you a taxi." I turned away when Gael's hand clasped around my wrist, hurting me. "I want you to come home with me."

"It's over." I pulled away, but he didn't release his grip. His expression resembled an angry mask. He looked like he'd drag me behind him all the way to the airport.

Thrain lunged at him and sent him flying against the couch. They both landed on the floor with a thud, Gael on his back and Thrain on top of him, his fists clenched around Gael's shirt. Given his short temper, I thought Gael would at least attempt to strike Thrain, but he just raised his hand, palms stretched out.

"I'm sorry, man. I didn't know you two were—" Gael's eyes gleamed with something, and for a moment I thought I saw that black glint again that seemed to shine through every now and then. It was gone in the blink of an eye.

Thrain got up and moved away from him, only to stop in front of me as though to protect me. I was slowly starting to get into this alpha thing. It sure was sexy as hell but so not appropriate right now.

"Go away." I pushed him aside and reached out to help Gael up.

"Thanks." He stood but didn't touch my hand. "A taxi would be great."

I nodded and hurried out into the hall, eager to escape the pained expression on his face. To dump him was one thing, but to let him see me with my new conquest just a day after breaking up was another. I felt horrible for doing this to him when he had stood by me after my sister's death.

"Let me help you," Amber whispered, taking the phone receiver out of my hand. I nodded thankfully and pressed my back against the wall. My feelings of guilt and shame threatened to choke me, and yet I knew there was nothing I could do to soften the blow. Gael was a catch. Every girl would be happy to date him. Just not me.

Gael appeared in the doorway. Amber put down the receiver and said to no one in particular, "A taxi will be here in an hour."

"So you're staying?" Gael asked. I didn't need to look up to know he was talking to me. I nodded. He took a deep breath. "Okay. Come to think of it, I won't need the ride. I forgot I told the taxi driver to wait down the street. Goodbye, Sofia." The melancholy in his voice cut a big hole in my heart.

221

"Take care." My eyes searched his. I thought I would find something there, maybe love or sadness, but there was nothing like it. For a moment, his lips curled into a smile—and not a nice one. A glint appeared in his eyes again, giving him a menacing look that made me flinch. A shiver ran down my spine.

And then he turned and disappeared with Aidan following behind probably to escort him out. For the first time, I breathed out, relieved and happy to see Gael go.

"You okay?" Amber asked.

I nodded and straightened my back. A feeling of urgency grabbed hold of me, as though I knew I didn't have much time left to finish what I had started. "Let's go back to the library, shall we?"

Amber seemed taken aback but didn't comment as she accompanied me, then disappeared to get the others. I stared out the window at the woods stretching behind the house. The crow was there again, regarding me intently, its beak slightly open. And then the screeching in my head resumed.

Chapter 20

Gael still lingered at the back of my mind when I took my previous spot on the couch. Cass had returned and sat next to me, her hands clasped around mine, her green, cat-like eyes shining. "Thank you for everything," she said, grabbing me in a tight hug.

I nodded, not used to gratefulness and open displays of affection coming from strangers, but I figured Cass and I weren't quite strangers, more like acquaintances and hopefully friends very soon. I barely knew her, but there was something about her that made me want to keep her around.

"How's Dallas?" Amber asked.

"He's sleeping. Now that his soul's returned to his body, Dad has arranged for our best healers to get him back in shape in no time."

"That's awesome," I said. Amber nodded. I could see her relief.

Cass blew her nose and wiped a hand over her cheeks. "You've no idea how much your help means to me." I didn't want to point out I never offered my help. They had actually kidnapped me in order to make a deal. And the deal had been a tempting one. She could read my mind anyway, so I'm pretty sure she got the message loud and clear. I smiled and let her continue, "I promised you would get to see Theo if you helped Dallas. You kept your part of the bargain, and now it's time for me to keep mine."

I took a deep breath and shot Thrain a hopeful look. He smiled at me encouragingly, then nodded. "I'm ready," I said, meaning every word. Hundreds of thoughts raced through my mind. How would I see my sister? Would Amber summon her from the otherworld? Would Cass be opening a portal so I could peer in? Or would someone play vessel? Wringing my hands in my lap, I smiled at myself, happy to finally get to see, hear or feel my sister again. It meant the world to me.

Cass flicked her phone open and typed in some numbers. The air began to crackle as though charged with electricity. A moment later, I felt a pull on my left arm that hung over the couch.

"Chop chop. We only have a minute before this thing closes, and I can't guarantee it will open again any time soon." Cass grabbed my arm to pull me up. Her grip was gentle, slightly impatient, but not forceful. I wondered whether the resurrection of her mate meant she had lost her reaper abilities.

"Yep," Cass said, grinning. "Can't pretend I'm not happy. While it might be fun to *fly* to places, those wings on my back weighted a ton. Another week and I would've resembled a Pterosaurs." When she noticed my confused expression, she laughed. "Doesn't ring a bell? They're, like, big, winged dinosaurs. Fast and strong, and deadly." Thrain said she used to be bubbly prior to her transformation. I could certainly see that now as Cass kept chatting.

Aidan pinched her biceps, winking at me. "Don't worry, Cass. You're nowhere near." She slapped his hand away, smiling, then motioned me to follow. I stood and stepped through the portal into...sizzling heat.

A hot gust blew my hair into my face, reminding me of popping my hands into an oven to pull out a hot dish, except that the temperature here was so high I almost expected my skin to melt. Cass pointed at the cracking, black earth under our feet. The fissures were the size of my forearm with white steam rising out of them.

"Aw, can't believe I've missed this place," Cass said.

"Me too," Amber said. "I kinda liked our tiny house in Distros."

Thrain leaned in to explain. "That's the second highest dimension of Hell." I felt my eyes widen. Then again, why was I even surprised? If the view didn't scream scorching heat, which doesn't quite fit the idea of Heaven, the smell certainly did.

I didn't need another confirmation that Hell existed, and I hoped—prayed—Theo wouldn't be here forever. I covered my nose to escape the biting stench of sulfur and forced myself to breathe through my open mouth.

"It's coming from the volcanoes over there." Cass pointed behind us to the hills in the distance. I gaped in awe at the huge mountains and the red sky. Foul-smelling gases seemed to shimmer in the setting sun. Bright orange magma erupted from the top, spreading in a wide circle like a huge halo, then flowed down at a leisurely speed, leaving a trail of liquid lava in its wake.

"Let's go. Dad's waiting," Cass said, taking off down what seemed to be a path, but I couldn't be sure because it was covered in dust and dry twigs and branches. We passed a large formation of boulders. The farther we marched through this deserted place, the faster Cass seemed to move. By the time we reached a tall fence, almost a foot taller than me, rivulets of sweat trickled down my body.

Cass opened the gate and let us into a large yard with yet more dying trees and a wilted lawn. My gaze wandered past the cobblestone path to the imposing building stretching against the sky. It was the biggest mansion I had ever seen, all red brick with huge bay windows and pretty turrets on the roof. Stretching up the walls were vines and rosebushes with thorns as large as my thumb. But what caught my attention were the stone gargoyles peering at us through eyes as black as coal. Feeling watched, I inched closer to Thrain, who wrapped his arm around me, and I swear for a moment I thought one of the gargoyles turned his head to follow me. Its lips pulled back to reveal fletched, razor sharp teeth. One of them shifted slowly and let out a piercing shriek.

"Spooky, huh?" Thrain whispered. "You should see them at night when their eyes turn red and fluorescent. They look like the miniature of Cass's hellhound. That one's not a pretty sight either."

"Are they alive?" My gaze settled on them. I almost expected them to jump down from their crouching position, spread their huge wings, and lunge at me to sink their teeth into my flesh.

"Very much so," Thrain said. "They're demons of a lower order with the sole purpose to protect the Big Boss." Aka the green-eyed guy I had seen after reuniting Dallas's soul with his body.

The huge mahogany door opened before us, freaking me out a bit. Cass motioned us to follow her into the tiled hall with several vases with fresh tulips. The walls were kept in an understated white, the only picture on the wall showed a young girl with red, braided hair and an infectious smile leaning over a huge, dog-like creature with a head so large it could probably swallow the child in one whole piece.

"*That's* her pet?" I whispered.

Thrain nodded, amused. "Yep. Don't ask to cuddle it though 'cause it's known to bite off a limb or two."

I puffed. Cuddling this beast was the last thing on my mind. In fact, the picture would probably haunt me in my dreams for the next few months. We followed Cass through a door to our left into a modern living room kept in yet more white with gray and red. In the middle of the room, leather couches were set up around a glass table in front of a fireplace. Black and white paintings with silver frames built a strong contrast to the blood red carpet covering the marble floor. Polished silver candleholders sparkled in the soft glow falling in through the windows covering the entire wall. It looked understated and yet so chic, I could swear it had been copied out of a magazine.

"Like it?" Cass smiled. I nodded enthusiastically, truly meaning it.

"Whoever designed this has amazing taste," I said.

She giggled and turned to the door a moment before it burst open and a huge guy hurried in, covering the entire length of the room in two long strides. Thrain bowed deeply.

"Dad." Cass fell into his arms. He laughed and planted a kiss on her red hair. His twinkling green eyes fell on me, and for a moment I forgot to breathe. The guy was even more gorgeous than in my vision. His white shirt with just one fashionable button undone stretched over his bulging muscles. I stared at the way his black hair fell against his broad shoulders, wondering whether it was as soft and dense as it seemed.

"You're kidding me. What's wrong with you, guys? First Amber couldn't stop gawking and now you," Cass said, peeling herself away from him. "Get a grip, mate. He's my *dad*. Do you have any idea how old he is? Like, ancient."

"Sofia. I'm Lucifer. Thank you for saving my daughter. I'll be forever in your debt." He inched forward and reached out his hand. I grabbed it in a slack grip, lost for words because I had never imagined the devil to be so—

"Gorgeous, handsome, fit?" Cass rolled her eyes, then turned to peer out the door. "Where's Dallas?"

"You mean this young man?" Lucifer stepped aside to free the view onto the hall. In the doorway stood the blond guy from my vision, his hands were buried deep in his pockets. A hesitant smile played on his lips. His wounds were gone, leaving a red scar behind.

The voodoo ritual had worked, which was proof I could tap into my powers and help a lost soul find his way back to his body. I looked at Cass expectantly, waiting for her to rush for him and give him the same enthusiastic greeting she had given her father, but she didn't. Instead, her lips began to quiver and tears streamed down her face. I could only hope it was the joy that froze her to the spot.

"I'm sorry, Dallas," she finally said.

He inched closer and wrapped his arms around her. A sob escaped her throat. The air was charged

229

with tension. Who knew reunions could be as difficult as goodbyes?

"I'm so sorry," she said for the umpteenth time. "For lying, for deceiving, for misleading you. I would never have done it were it not for this stupid curse."

"That will bind you to Hell until you marry your soulmate," he finished the sentence, wiping her tears off her cheeks. "I knew you were lying, Cass. Your whole story didn't make much sense. I just thought you would start telling the truth at some point, you know, for the sake of our relationship. But you never did, until it was too late."

Watching Cass crying, I realized how fragile she was when I thought she was the strongest of us. Dallas pulled her against his chest and whispered soothing words I couldn't discern. Eventually, Cass's crying subsided and she turned away from him, still holding his hand as though she feared she would lose him again.

"Dallas," Amber called out.

He noticed us then. The way his eyes sparkled, I could see his joy at reuniting with his sister. "Hey, sis. What's with the pale as a ghost look? I thought I was the goner." Grinning, he pointed at her pale face and grabbed her in a tight hug. It was a happy reunion that reminded me I still hadn't seen my sister, but I didn't want to spoil their special moment.

"Great job, Sofia." Lucifer nodded and disappeared behind one of the big doors, only to reappear a few seconds later.

"What's so funny?" Cass said. My attention snapped back to her.

Dallas shook his head. "Nothing."

"You don't believe this curse exists. You think I made it up." Her voice betrayed reproach and a very short temper.

Dallas raised his hands in mock defense. " Of course I believe you. It's just that your birthday is in less than a week."

"Thanks for pointing out that you're not ready to marry me," she scoffed. I peered from Amber to Cass and then back to Amber whose expression mirrored my thoughts.

She whispered to me, "Trouble in paradise, and this after five minutes together. Isn't love grand?"

I had no idea what that curse entailed, but I could tell whatever it was the guy had no intention to marry her. I felt sorry for Cass. Lying wasn't exactly a desirable trait, but whatever fibs she had told him couldn't be so bad when she had just saved his life.

"Go out and enjoy your last days of freedom," Dallas said. "I'll be here, waiting for you."

"You're such a moron." Amber marched over and punched his shoulder. "Why don't you just marry her? You share a bond, you idiot, and she just saved your life. The least you could do is get rid of that commitment phobia of yours and tie the knot."

I nodded, even though I lacked the background knowledge and the whole situation wasn't even my business.

"She's right, Dallas," Aidan said.

"I never said I wouldn't marry her," Dallas said. "Just not now. I want us to get to know each other without all the lies and the deceit, which is why I'm staying here with you." His hand brushed Cass's hair out of her face. "Are you listening? I'm not going anywhere. Just no more lying, Cass."

Her hand clenched and unclenched. As the Princess of Darkness Cass was probably used to getting her way, so someone defying her wishes wasn't helping her short temper.

"Cass?" Lucifer said. The warning in his voice didn't go unnoticed. Her shoulders slumped slightly, but her fists remained clenched.

"I need a timeline. How long am I supposed to stay here, locked up in this *prison*?" she asked.

Dallas shook his head, grinning. "As long as it takes."

"No."

"I'm ready to negotiate...in private." He grabbed her arm and pulled her into the hall, disappearing with her down the hall.

"Just don't try to do anything funny. I can still hear you," Lucifer yelled after them. I thought it was just a joke, until he turned and I noticed his dead serious expression. "I believe you came here for something in particular."

My palms started to sweat. A shiver ran down my spine. Thrain wrapped his arm around my shoulder to steady me, misinterpreting my sudden shaking.

"Theo! Care to join us?" Lucifer's voice sounded soft and tender, like a father speaking to a child.

I craned my neck to get a better glimpse at the fourteen year old girl appearing in the hall. Her long, flowing, white dress gave her the appearance of an angel floating above the ground. Her blonde hair looked like a glowing curtain, reaching down to her waist.

My breath caught in my throat as I reached out for her to close her in my arms. She felt so tiny and fragile, so lost. Huge sobs rippled the air. It took me a while to realize they were my own.

"They said I could see you soon, but I never believed it," Theo whispered, wiping away the tears covering my cheeks.

I laughed through my ebbing sobs. "For the last six months I've been wanting to tell you how sorry I am for what happened."

"It wasn't your fault. I shouldn't have been so careless," Theo whispered. Yes, that was my sister, always blaming herself.

From the corner of my eye, I watched the others pouring out of the room and the door closing behind them. I sat down on the couch with Theo in my arms, my hands brushing her soft, almost white hair as we lost ourselves in a long talk, recalling the past to fill in

the blanks that had always made me doubt Theo's
death had been an accident.

Chapter 21

Seven months earlier

It was the beginning of January. Only a few days ago, we had celebrated Christmas together. Sitting on the plush couch between my father and his new wife, Marie had been an awkward affair, considering that the woman had split up my family when I was just a child, and taken my father away from my mother. I felt the usual guilt nagging at the back of mind, but more than ever I was determined to ignore it. As much as I blamed my father and his new wife for giving up the life he had shared with us, he was trying hard to make me forget his betrayal by helping me with my music career.

Since the day I mentioned I wanted to be a musician, he paid for months of intensive voice training. Marie even organized a gig for me. It wasn't a big one, just some minor two-song performance in a well-known club in Manhattan. But apparently a scout would attend, which turned what should've been a nice experience into a huge opportunity that made my heart race.

I wiped my damp hands on my short skirt as I slipped into my boots and leather jacket, then hugged my half-sister, Theo, tight. Even though we didn't grow up together, we had always been close. Surprisingly, I had never blamed her for my father's choice to leave my mother and me behind to start a new life with Marie and their daughter, Theo. Maybe because she had always looked up to me like a real sister.

"Good luck, Soph. You know you won't need it 'cause you'll blow them away." Her thin voice betrayed her nervousness. She knew how much this meant to me and she tried her best to boost my confidence.

"Thanks." I kissed her cheek and grabbed my guitar case. "Don't wait up."

"Are you kidding me? I'll wait up and I'll want to know *everything*," Theo said. Smiling, I gave her a last squeeze, then hurried out the door.

Darkness had descended half an hour ago. The winter wind whipped my hair into my face. I pulled my hood over my head and marched down the busy street in search of a taxi. I knew I should've called one to wait outside the building, but I figured it would take less than five minutes to find one. After all, this was New York with a taxi around every corner. Or so I thought.

Ten minutes later, I was still squeezing my way through busy post-Christmas sale shoppers, who had gathered in front of the fashion outlets littering this part of the city. Several taxis had swooshed past, all occupied or unwilling to stop. My fingers were frozen in my mittens, the cold in my toes felt like icicles. I reached into my almost empty bag and realized I forgot my cell phone, meaning calling a taxi was out of the question.

Having spent a few months in Manhattan I knew my way around, so I wrapped my jacket tighter around my shivering body to fight the cold and battled forward against the wind. In the darkness, all streets looked the same. It took me a while to realize I was lost.

"Crap." I stomped my foot impatiently as I tried to read the street sign in the distance. I had left the house early because I wanted to avoid making a beginner mistake like arriving late and blowing my chance. But my watch told me time was running out. If I didn't hurry, I would indeed make the biggest mistake of my life. Just as I didn't expect it, a taxi drove around the corner. I waved and yelled, even though I doubted the driver could hear me. My heart started to beat like a drum in my ears as the vehicle drove past—and pulled over. I ran the short distance and jumped onto the backseat, telling the driver I was in a hurry. The driver sped off before I even closed the door.

The streets were unusually busy. Leaning against the cold leather, I could already tell I wouldn't make it on time. My spirits dropped as my future rolled like a black and white movie before my eyes. Would I ever get such a chance again? I didn't think so.

I arrived at the bar an hour late, paid the driver and got out. For a short moment, I still hoped I might get a chance to play after all—until I saw the blue lights flashing in the parking space and people gathered around an ambulance. Two police officers were trying to disperse the crowd.

"What happened?" I asked a girl standing nearby.

"Someone was killed right outside the club," she said.

"That's horrible." A cold shiver ran down my spine and my hands turned clammy at the thought of a murderer running berserk. "I hope they got the killer." I craned my head to get a better view at the victim, catching a glimpse of her blonde hair. Before the doors of the ambulance car slammed shut, I recognized the familiar face. A chilling scream pierced my eardrums—a scream I realized was mine.

"Theo!" I screamed, pushing through the crowd.

A police officer pushed me back. "Please step back, Ma'am."

"That's my sister," I screamed, my tears blurring my sight. He shook his head, signaling he wouldn't let me through, and the ambulance drove away. I broke down, crying. Someone helped me to my feet and said something. I pushed the person away from me, devastated. I would never mistake that white blonde curtain of hair, and yet denial kicked in. Maybe it wasn't Theo. It couldn't be.

A thick haze descended upon my mind as I wandered through the streets for hours. I don't know how I made it back home, only that my father and Marie were already there with a female police officer. Marie was crying against my father's chest as he tried to comfort her. I had never seen so much rage on his face, but the incident still didn't quite register with me. I felt as though I was watching a tragic show on television.

"You must be Sofia," the officer said. I nodded and sat down on the couch. The police officer's face remained dead serious as she continued, "I'll need to ask you a few questions, please."

"It's all your fault," Marie screamed, her face contorted in agony, palms pressed against her chest as she sobbed. "If it weren't for you, she'd still be alive."

"Shush." My father drew Marie to his chest, but I could see the reproach in his eyes. They thought me responsible for Theo's death, and somehow I felt as though they were right. She must've followed me to that club and if it were not for my performance, she would still be here.

***

Still sitting on Cass's couch cradling my baby sister Theo in my arms, I wiped the tears from my eyes as I listened to Theo's story.

She said I had barely left her parents' house when the phone rang. The club manager called to inform me the scout would arrive half an hour early and I would have to hurry to make it. Theo immediately called my cell number only to hear it ring where I had left it on the breakfast table in the hall. Unsure how else to reach me, she called a taxi from my cell phone, told her parents she'd be going to bed early and sneaked out of the house.

She arrived at the club before me and since she was underage and they wouldn't let her wait inside, she thought it best to wait near the car park until I arrived. She had been freezing in the cold for a few minutes when movement caught her attention. From the corner of her eye, she noticed Derrick, Gael's brother, behind her. She wasn't scared because we had spent many days in Central Park together, and she trusted him. Before she could turn around, his palm clamped around her mouth, muffling her startled yelp.

Theo recounted how she kicked and tried to break free from his iron lock when he dragged her behind a car and thrust a knife into her chest several times. The excruciating pain cut off her air support. Blood poured out of her, gathering in a puddle on the ground and making her dizzy. She raised her gaze to meet his dark eyes.

240

"Theo?" He kneeled beside her and gathered her in his arms. "I'm so sorry. I didn't know. I thought—"

In the dim light of a streetlamp she could hear the gurgling sound in her throat. She opened her mouth to speak and spit out a warm, thick liquid. A dark figure grabbed Derrick's arm and tried to pull him away from her, muttering something she didn't understand. Derrick dropped her limp body to the ground together with the knife. She knew she was dying, but it wasn't right. Her time shouldn't have come yet. Anger rose inside her. Pushing up on her elbows, Theo's gaze focused on Derrick. She picked up the knife and, with her last might, she plunged it into his neck before darkness descended upon her. Derrick's scream for help pierced her eardrum a moment before he was dragged away. The image before her eyes became blurry, then dissipated into nothing. As a sense of peace washed over her, Theo dropped back onto the asphalt. Pitch black gathered around her, enveloping her a spilt second later, and she let go of life willingly, happy to have avenged her death.

Chapter 22

The door opened and closed with a soft click. My arms were still wrapped around Theo's shivering body; a sob escaped my throat even though I had long depleted all tears.

"I'm so sorry," Thrain's voice whispered in my ear. His hand wrapped around my shoulders to help me up. I didn't want to leave my sister, but I knew my time with her was probably up. As I peered up at Thrain, I could see the moisture glistening in his eyes, as if he had been crying with me. "Ready to go?" he asked.

I shook my head. "I'll never be."

He wrapped his arm around my waist and shot Theo a smile. "I know, but we'll take good care of her." The thought comforted me for all of three seconds.

"Gael's brother, Derrick, killed her," I said.

"I know." His voice was so gentle, it broke my heart. I felt tears pricking my eyes again. Thrain squeezed my hand. "I'm sorry, I've been instructed to take you home. Take your time saying goodbye. I'll wait outside."

I nodded and grabbed Theo in a tight hug again, whispering words of comfort I needed just as much. Even though I had discovered how she had died and who the killer was, I wished I also knew his motive.

Derrick had died of a heart attack at around the same time as Theo—or so Gael's family said. I had felt sorry for them, but I no longer did. Whatever fate befell him, he deserved it. I hoped he rotted in Hell this very instant.

It took me a while to peel myself away from Theo and say goodbye to her and Cass's father, who hugged me before sending me back through the portal into the real world. My work was done, and yet Amber and Aidan insisted I spend some time with them in Scotland before returning to New York. Immediate solitude would've been my first choice but my Russian roots prohibited me from snubbing hospitality, particularly since these people were my friends now, and they meant well.

When we arrived back at Aidan's mansion, night had already descended upon the Scottish Highlands. I wasn't hungry so I excused myself and went to bed early, eager to hide under the blanket and be alone with my thoughts and pain. I took a quick shower and slipped into a pair of Amber's flannel PJs, ready to switch off the lights, when a knock on the door jolted me out of my thoughts.

"Are you decent?" Thrain's voice made my heart pick up in speed.

"Yep. Come in." I smiled as he entered and wiggled a bottle of wine and two glasses in the air.

"You don't need to talk if you don't want to. Just pay me company." His gorgeous smile revealed shiny, white teeth.

"Can't be on your own, huh?" I asked, patting the bed beside me.

"I'm a bit embarrassed to admit it, but darkness scares me." He poured us a glass of wine and handed me one. I took it from his outstretched hand but didn't drink. Surprisingly, he didn't insist. Not even when I placed the glass on the bedside table.

"Or you're trying to get me drunk." My gaze wandered over the tight shirt that enveloped his sculpted chest. His rolled up sleeves revealed strong forearms with smooth, tan skin. My fingers brushed his hand and moved up his arm as I inched closer, stopping just as our lips were about to meet. I could see the hunger in his striking green gaze. In his mind, he was probably undressing me this instant. I had dated other guys but never felt such a strong need to get close to someone.

"Kiss me." My voice was barely more than a whisper. His lips lowered onto mine, his hand moved to my back to press me against him. A soft moan escaped my throat as his scent invaded my nostrils.

My hands moved up his chest to the back of his head to pull him closer into our kiss. I savored his taste, got lost in it, forgetting the pain inside me. It felt so good, and I knew he felt the same way. He understood me because we were the same, maybe not one and the same being but bonded through something beyond our understanding. This guy I would never let go.

He pulled away, ending our kiss too soon. I moaned in protest. He lowered me on my back, regret visible in his heated gaze.

"Don't stop," I whispered.

"Another time." His finger pressed against my lips. "Please don't insist. I'm having a hard time keeping my hands off of you."

That I wanted to see. I giggled and pinched his side, then wrapped my naked legs around his waist to draw him close.

"You didn't just do that," he said, grinning. His eyes twinkled as he lowered himself on top of me for another kiss. This time it was slower, deeper, making me want to trail my hand down his naked chest to explore the tattoo he kept hidden. Kissing me deeply, his hands moved down my abdomen to my thighs, lingering there.

"I don't think this is a good idea," Thrain said, pulling back a bit.

"What?" I pulled him closer again, my mouth searching his. I could feel his hot breath grazing my skin. He nibbled on the spot right at the bottom of my neck that connected with my shoulder, making me shivered.

"Actually, I came to talk," he said, hoarsely.

"Figured that much." I smiled because, when a guy says he wants to talk, it usually means he either wants more but tries to control himself, or he's about to dump the girl. I was pretty sure it was option one and ran my fingers through his hair to draw him close. But he sat up and put a few more inches between us.

"We really need to talk about this." His grave tone betrayed resolution. Now, that wasn't good news. I moistened my lips. Panic washed over me. I had been dumped before and had done my fair share of dumping, but somehow in this instance it mattered. Maybe I had too much emotional baggage and he couldn't handle it. I knew I shouldn't have cried in front of him. According to a magazine article I recently read, most men were put off by tears.

I crossed my legs and pulled my shirt down to cover my naked skin. "Okay. Spill."

He regarded me for a long time, his eyes darting about, never quite focusing on my gaze. "You said you wanted to return home." I nodded. My heart sank in my chest as I waited for him to continue. "I told you my job makes it almost impossible to be in one place for a long time. I don't know how this will work out."

There it was—the dumping I hadn't seen coming. The guy was giving me the boot an hour after I had learned about my sister's mysterious death. Rage pulsed through me. I wished I didn't care, but I did.

After all, he was the one who said we'd always together. *Lies,* my mind screamed. "No worries. I'll be busy with my music career anyway," I heard myself say. My voice was steady and nonchalant, betraying none of the turmoil I felt inside.

Frowning, Thrain shook his head. "That's not what I meant, Sofia. I want this, but we'll need to figure something out. I don't want you to be all alone in New York with me popping in and out of your life every few days. That's not a relationship."

I took a deep breath as relief washed over me. Funny how a few words from this guy could change my mood in an instant.

"We'll figure something out," I said, wrapping my arms around him. "Let's not think about it now. We have plenty of time left."

He hesitated, then gave into my embrace, lowering his lips onto mine. I lay back and pulled him on top of me as I let his mouth explore mine. My hands trailed down his stomach, sliding underneath his shirt to take it off. I touched the outline of his tattoo that covered most of his chest. His skin felt like silk under my exploring fingers. Half naked, he was more gorgeous than I ever imagined.

"You're so beautiful," he whispered as his hands moved under my shirt. I closed my eyes to enjoy his expert touch. As much as my music career mattered to me, if being with him meant giving it up I'd let it go gladly. I had lost my sister over my career already; I wouldn't let it happen twice.

247

Chapter 23

Thrain didn't stay the night. At some point I woke up and patted the sheet to find he had left. Had it been a mistake to get closer to him? Did he now think I was easy to get? Too late for that, I figured, angry with myself for not even giving him a bit of a chase. Disappointed, I punched the pillow and stood up to pull the curtains, which I forgot to draw.

The moon stood high on the horizon, bathing the woods stretching over the hills in a glowing hue. It was so pretty and quiet, so different to the usual New York view of illuminated skyscrapers and dark asphalt streets. I decided I might not get to see something this spectacular any time soon and left the curtains open after all. Even though Amber's flannel PJs were the warmest I had ever had, I grabbed my sweater from the back of the chair and put it on, then returned to my cozy bed, ready to catch some much needed snooze, with or without Thrain sleeping beside me.

Pulling my cover up to my chin, I barely closed my eyes when the door opened and footsteps thudded across the carpet, stopping next to my side of the bed. I snuggled under the blanket and smiled because he hadn't left after all. Maybe he just needed to use the restroom, or woke him, forcing him to get a midnight snack. Even demons had to eat every now and then. When he continued to hover there, I groaned inwardly. Granted, love was a grand thing, making one all fluffy and warm, but his staring was slowly starting to make me feel uncomfortable. Besides, I needed someone to keep me warm and cozy. I pushed the covers aside whispering, "Come on already." He didn't budge.

The strange feeling in the pit of my stomach intensified. Something wasn't right, so I opened my eyes. The moonlight falling in through the high bay window caught on something shiny. And then I realized what it was: a knife. My eyes widened as I rolled to the other side of the bed a moment before the blade cut open my pillow. Jumping up from the bed, I dashed for the door when he gripped my hair and pulled me back. The pain rippling through my scalp was excruciating.

"Thrain, you're hurting me," I screamed. I couldn't believe he had turned all psycho on me. Yelping, I kicked hard, hitting the guy right where it hurt the most, then stood and took off down the hall and stairs. A groan and thuds echoed not far behind me, but I didn't turn. My fear kept me running.

The house was dark. No sound that would betray anyone's presence. I couldn't believe how naive I was for trusting a guy I met less than a week ago. Come to think of it, what did I actually know about him? He was a demon and they usually came with a bit of a tendency toward murder, or so legends said. My heart hammered hard in my chest as I headed for the kitchen. I couldn't remember whether the door could be locked from the inside, but I figured if there was no key, I stood a better chance hiding in the woods than inside the house with a killer searching for me. My hands patted the lock only to find there was no key. Damn it.

I opened the backdoor and took off into the night like the wind, making sure I closed the door behind me in case the guy followed. My breathing made a whistling sound as I shimmied through the bushes and trees, not paying attention to the cold that crept up my legs and turned my skin into goose bumps. I ran for a few minutes before I dared to look over my shoulder. The trees looked like huge, ominous shapes in the darkness. Stopping, I pressed my back against a thick trunk and held my breath to listen. Nothing stirred. I got rid of him. Now what? I couldn't return back to the house, but just my flannel PJs and sweater wouldn't be able to keep me warm against the cold for long. Sooner or later, I would freeze to death.

A twig snapped to my right. I turned my head sharply. Only too late did I see the dark shadow from the corner of my eye. Something hard hit my temple, sending me flying into a bush. I groaned and pushed up on my elbows, paralyzed with fear, the pain banging against my skull making me dizzy.

"Hey, are you looking for me?"

My head shot up at the familiar sound of my own voice. How did I speak when my mouth never opened? I hadn't even formed the words in my mind. And then I saw her standing near a tree. The moonlight caught in her dyed black hair and made her pale face look even paler. She wore a white flannel shirt that hung down to her knees, rolled up at the sleeves to reveal thin forearms. My breath caught in my throat. She was the spitting image of me. Even her nightwear looked like what I was wearing. But how could it be, unless I was dead and looking at my own body? But shouldn't my body be lying on the ground with me hovering over it instead of the other way round? My stomach turned. I felt so dizzy from all the pounding inside my head, I feared I'd be throwing up any minute.

"Sofia? I've been looking for you," the figure standing a few feet away from me said. I turned my head, seeing Gael standing there. The tip of his knife was inches away from my throat. Scared, I peered from him to the girl, who looked like me, and then back to Gael.

"What are you doing, Gael? Why did you hit her?" the girl asked in a thin voice that betrayed her fear. She inched closer and reached out to touch Gael's arm. The air crackled and a tiny spark flew from his skin. Frowning, she pulled her hand back.

"I didn't hit your friend. She fell," Gael said. "It's freezing out here. Come on, let me take you home." Gael reached for me and yanked me up by my arm, sending a pang of pain through my already aching body. Dragging me behind him, he took a few slow steps toward her, his blade still lingering near my neck. Who was the girl? Where did she come from? And most importantly, why did she look like me? I couldn't make any sense of the whole situation, and yet I could tell something wasn't right. Gael wasn't here to help me—or her. Not when he wielded a knife. I opened my mouth to warn her when she turned her gaze toward me, and I saw something there. A flicker, like that of a television set with bad reception. For a fragment of a second, the girl's face seemed to shift, only to turn back into my spitting image. Lost for words, I closed my mouth again and remained silent.

"You're cold," Gael said. "My car's nearby. I'll drive you back to the house."

"Thank you," she whispered. "It's freezing out here." Her gaze moved from Gael to the knife in his hand, hesitating again.

"You're coming with us," Gael whispered to me. "We wouldn't want you to freeze to death." The girl didn't comment. "You lead the way," Gael said to her. She nodded grimly and started walking.

Gael's hand clasped around my elbow as he guided me forward. His other hand still held on to his knife, knuckles turned white. Walking back to the house would've been the better choice instead of trekking through the woods, and yet Gael seemed to move us away from it. The farther we trekked, the more I knew we were in danger, but could two women take out a guy with a knife? I had never been particularly strong and she didn't look like a bodybuilder either. I knew if I ran he'd catch me in a heartbeat, what with my spinning head and my frozen body that could barely move. Time to come up with a plan, and fast, before something bad happened. I peered around me for a weapon that I could use. Maybe a large stone or a thick branch to knock him over the head with. If I could swing a guitar, I sure could swing a branch to take down a guy.

"Over here." Gael pointed to a large black vehicle that blended into the night. A gust of wind blew the scent of incense and lavender into my face. I followed Gael down the incline and stopped in my tracks. Behind the vehicle was a large circle with stones set up to mark the edges. In the middle, branches and dried herbs formed a large nest, like that of a bird.

"What the—" My voice caught in my throat as the guy knocked me to the ground, then grabbed hold of my long hair and dragged me to the middle of the circle. I let out a shriek and tried to grab hold of his wrist to push him away.

"Did you really think I'd fall for your cheap trick, witch? All those months playing your friend weren't for nothing," he hissed as he pushed me to the ground. Tiny gravel cut through my PJs and grazed my skin. I tried to crawl away but he grabbed hold of my leg and pulled me back in, twisting my ankle in the process. It was the same one I twisted while running away from Devon not long ago. I cried out in pain as tears filled my eyes.

"Hey, I'm Sofia. Let her go," the girl shouted.

"If you're Sofia, why don't you enter the circle?" Gael's tone betrayed his arrogance. Anger rose inside me, making me want to slap that grin from his face. The girl lunged forward only to fall back as soon as she hit the invisible barrier around the circle. Gael laughed. "No? Didn't think so. Because only the real witch could enter. Whatever you are, you're no match for me."

The girl growled, and for a moment her face began to flicker again as she lunged forward, throwing herself against the invisible shield around the circle, only to be thrown back. I could see the frustration on her face, the frown lines on her forehead, the rage in her eyes. She kept circling the invisible shield, throwing herself against it in the hope to find a weak spot, but she couldn't enter. My gaze moved back to Gael. Madness glittered in his eyes, and I knew I had to stall for time if I wanted to live.

"Why did you take me to see Madame Estevaz?"

My question took him by surprise. He smiled. "She was supposed to see your past to make sure you were Esmeralda's incarnation, but she failed me. Unfortunately for her, a betrayal doesn't go unpunished in my family."

"Why did you kill her?" I remembered the dark entity around me, clutching my soul, marking me. Was it the same one that had taken my life all those years ago?

"She had to die because she recognized you. Said she wouldn't help me kill a priestess, so she triggered your memories so you could use your powers." Gael grinned. "They aren't much use to you now, huh?" His raised his blade over his head.

I struggled to get up as panic gripped hold of me. My gaze fell on the sharp metal engraved with silver symbols. Maybe he wasn't all bad and had an excuse like finding out about my abilities and thinking I might be able to resurrect his brother. I moistened my lips to gather my voice. "Please, if you want to talk to Derrick I have friends who can help."

"Derrick was an idiot," Gael hissed. "He whacked the wrong Romanov witch. Luckily, little Theo did the job I should've done a long time ago."

"You wanted to kill your brother?"

"I should have," Gael said. "He almost messed up my big chance. You see, legend says only the Blade of Sorrow can kill you, but we hadn't found it yet. Not without a bounty hunter's help. He wouldn't wait so he tried any knife before I could stop him. He said it would work and I believed him. Theo and you looked so similar, the same height with your long, blonde hair. The moment Theo died, I knew he had the wrong sister."

I hadn't dyed my hair black yet, and it had been dark that fateful January night. Mixing us up made sense. A pang of guilt surged through me. So my stepmother, Marie, was right. Theo's death was my fault. If I took a taxi and didn't arrive late, Theo would still be alive. The rage I had been nourishing for the last few months turned against him, against myself, against fate for being so cruel and letting me make such a stupid mistake.

"You said he almost messed up your big chance," I said. "The chance for what?"

"Your powers."

I raised my chin, sensing my chance to escape the psycho. "You can have them. I'll give them to you willingly. Just let me go." Somewhere outside the circle I thought I could hear someone's voice—maybe the girl from before—but I couldn't let anything divert my attention, not with Gael being much stronger than me. Slacking in concentration wasn't an option if I wanted to make it out of this situation alive.

He shook his head, still grinning. "And how do you propose to do that?"

"I'll figure something out," I whispered.

"I have a better idea." He took a step forward, the blade in his hand shinning menacingly with the promise of a long and painful death. "I'll cut it out of you, and then I'll get what I want. What I deserve." Without so much as a warning, he lunged for me. I kicked, aiming for his abdomen, but only hit the air as he ducked out of the way. The blade hit my left shoulder and I cried out in pain. My fingers moved instinctively to the gash. For a moment I just stared, horrified, at the red liquid that shimmered almost black in the darkness, trickling down my arm. And then the real pain began. Pulsating pain that came in hot waves and seared my flesh. I bit my lip to keep myself conscious, but my vision was already blurry and my brain numb, threatening to descend into that darkness I kept seeing in my dreams. Death. Maybe the darkness had been a warning or a prophecy telling me what lay before me. My lungs burned as I breathed in and out the cold Scottish air. I begged my brain to remain lucid, but I knew I didn't have much time. I had to find a way to get away from him.

"Gael," a male voice called calmly. Gael turned his head at the resolute tone and I followed his line of vision to the Shadow, Devon, standing next to Thrain. The girl looking like me was gone. I had no idea where the two had come from and where the girl had disappeared. It was strange to see Thrain's beautiful face resemble an angry mask. As striking as Devon was, Thrain took my breath away even through the hazy curtain of pain surrounding me.

"I'm almost done," Gael whispered. His voice came raw, intense. I could sense the darkness in him, hurrying him along, and yet I knew he waited for something, but I didn't know what that something was.

"You'll always be a bastard, never one of us," Devon said, calmly.

"No." Gael shook his head and peered up at the low moon disappearing behind the clouds. "Once I have her powers, I can transport the Queen's soul into another Shadow's body. Her pain and suffering will be gone forever. I'll do it, I'll help her and then she'll let me join."

"She won't." Devon inched closer and pulled out a sword from under his cloak.

"Please help her. I'll do whatever you want," Thrain pleaded.

"Anything?" Devon asked.

Thrain nodded. "You have my word."

"A demon's word. I wonder what it's worth," Devon said, raising the sword over his head. I could see his lips moving, murmuring. The earth began to move under our feet.

"No!" Gael shouted. "You don't need her. She'll never join you, but I will." In that instant, a soft ray of light caught in his blade. It was the first ray of the rising sun Gael had been waiting for. He raised his blade higher and I could see he was ready to strike. My scream found its way out of my throat a moment before he brought the blade crashing down. My vision blurred. I felt dizzy and nauseous again, but it was nothing compared to the pain spreading through my body. The jerk had stabbed me, that was my last thought before darkness gathered around me.

Chapter 24

Pain rippled through my body in long pangs that made breathing difficult. My muscles contracted, the effort drenching me in sweat. From the periphery of my mind, I knew someone was around me, holding my hand, whispering soothing words in my ears, begging me to come back. I smiled because I remembered Thrain. Our kiss, our night together. It had been so special, so beautiful. I wanted it again, that perfect moment of hope and happiness that seared my heart and soul every time our gazes connected. So I held on and fought when that darkness threatened to pull me in.

When I finally opened my eyes, I squinted against the glaring brightness, wishing someone had thought of closing the curtains. And then I realized Thrain wasn't there. It was Devon standing next to my bed, dark and broody, dressed in his usual black attire.

Behind him, Aidan leaned against the wall. And next to him was a familiar face I couldn't immediately place. Tall guy with dark bed hair and blue eyes, Aidan's spitting image but a bit bulkier, clad in blue jeans and a crumpled shirt.

"She's awake," the guy whispered.

"Last time I checked no one was blind," Cass muttered from my right.

My head shot in her direction, surprised to find her here. And there he stood. Thrain. Right next to her. For a moment, I forgot to breathe as I lost myself in his impossibly green eyes. Smiling, I reached out for him. He grabbed my hand in a tight grip, placed a soft kiss on my palm, and leaned over me to whisper in my ear. "I was so scared I'd lose you."

"Fat chance." My raspy voice was barely audible in my ears. "How long have I been gone?"

"Too long. Now drink this." He held a glass of what looked like water to my lips. I took a few sips and grimaced at the bitter residue on my tongue.

"I'm so sorry," the dark guy with blue eyes said, drawing my attention to him. It took me a split second to remember where we had met. The garden behind our hotel in Rio de Janeiro. He had been the one to warn me. Kieran. How strange I didn't see the resemblance between Aidan and him straight away. Must have been because it was dark.

"You should be, moron. It's your fault she was almost killed," Cass hissed. "What's it with you and killing mortals? Must be a curse or something." She

261

turned to face me. "Sofia, this is Aidan's brother, Kieran McAllister, who must've inherited the stupidity in their clan." I nodded because I appreciated the introduction even if I didn't need it.

"How could I've known the weirdo intended to use the blade to murder someone?" Kieran said. "He claimed it was a collector's item."

"Collector's item, my ass," Aidan muttered. "A bounty hunter's job is to find out what the object's used for before retrieving it."

My head snapped from left to right as I tried to make sense of their words. Gael had employed Kieran to look for something. Could it be a blade?

"The Blade of Sorrow," Cass said, reading my mind as she shot Kieran a venomous look. "Every idiot could look up on the internet what it's good for. Seriously, with all the weird writing on it, did it *look* like a collector's item to you? You wouldn't even see it if it had a sticky note with the words 'ritual killing' attached to it." She smirked.

Her words triggered my memories. The stone circle and the rising sun, so beautiful and yet terrible. Gael wanting to spill my blood, claiming only the blade in his hands could kill me. Me knocking my head as I tried to escape that madman's blow.

"It's okay. I'm sure you had a reason." I smiled at poor Kieran who had so clearly been played, just like me.

"Sure, he does," Cass said. "Since big brother had to hide in Hell, money's been tight. Kieran had two

262

options, either get a day job like everyone else, or turn part-time crook and steal stuff. Do I need to point out which option he chose?"

"Bounty hunter," Kieran said through gritted teeth.

"Is that what you call it?" Cass asked, grinning. "Don't flatter yourself, mate. I'm outta here. Call you later, Soph." She kissed my cheek, then breezed out the door, the bright rays of sun falling in through the window catching in her red mane. I wondered whether by calling she actually meant popping over any time she wanted. I hoped she would.

"What happened to Gael?" I asked Devon. "Did you—"

"Kill him?" He raised his brows. "We don't kill our own kind, Sofia."

Nodding, I swallowed hard. They had no problem betraying others though. "So Gael's a Shadow?"

"Half Shadow. His mother was one of us. His father's something entirely else." He hesitated, and I wondered whether there was more to the story. Devon continued, not giving me a chance to pursue the matter. "He's been trying to take his place among our kind for years. He thought by killing you and passing your powers into our possession to save our Queen, we'd finally grant him entrance to our world."

Kieran snorted, interrupting him. "The guy's clearly messed up big time. Who in their right mind would want to join a legion of black eyed freaks with the personality of a freezer?" Aidan elbowed him in the ribs. Grinning, Kieran shrugged. "You're right.

I'm so sorry, I'm offending one of the greatest inventions of our time. Humanity would be lost without a freezer."

A dangerous glitter flickered in Devon's eyes, reminding me of the way Gael had looked at me many times during our relationship. "Let's get back to the topic before someone gets seriously hurt. There's no doubt he'll come back for you together with others, who'll want to use your powers for their own gain. I won't be there to protect you."

My heart sank in my chest at the implication of yet more danger. As though sensing my emotions, Thrain squeezed my hand. As my bonded mate, he would face it with me, I knew it. He didn't even need to say it. I raised my chin defiantly. Whatever fate had mapped out for me, I wasn't scared.

"Bring it on." My voice didn't sound quite as convincing as I intended to make it sound. "That reminds me, why are you even here? I thought you couldn't enter the property."

Aidan smirked. "He doesn't. Amber *invited* him. For some inexplicable reason, she still thinks his kind and the vampires should be burying our ancient misunderstandings."

"They weren't misunderstandings, only consequences," Devon said. "One of you killed half a dozen of us. I was there and remember the incident clearly."

"Dude, how old are you?" Kieran said, grinning. "If you start crumbling into dust I swear I'm not going to clean up after you."

Devon's jaw set. His serious expression betrayed the fight he was leading with himself. In the end, his shoulders tensed but he didn't take Kieran up on the offer of a brawl. "As he was saying," Devon continued, pointing at Aidan, "Amber invited me in to sit with you in case your wellbeing deteriorated. And I agreed wholeheartedly because your time hasn't come yet. Our rules state that no mortal soul shall come to harm at the hands of a Shadow." He leaned forward to look deep into my eyes. I flinched at the perfection of his features and the blackness of his gaze standing in contrast to the smooth, pale skin. "We want your soul, Sofia, make no mistake about that. And your soul will belong to the Cemetery of the Dead as arranged many centuries ago."

"Never," Thrain hissed, startling me. I patted his hand, my gaze begging him to keep his mouth shut and let Devon reveal his intentions. Knowing what to expect was the key to finding a way to get out of that binding contract I had signed centuries ago.

"Our Queen has never been wrong," Devon continued unfazed. His gaze glimmered black, daring Thrain to disagree.

I took a deep breath and squeezed Thrain's hand a bit harder to send out a warning. "My sister died at the hands of a Shadow, Gael's brother, Derrick. I bet you didn't know that, huh?" Anger rose inside me.

Why hadn't they been there to help her? Why would I deserve to live and not Theo?"

"Her time had come anyway. She'll be reincarnated," Devon said, coolly. It was a cheap excuse for not monitoring the lunatics among them, and I had no doubt many Shadows were marked by madness, what with their queen feeding from her own people, turning them into something unnatural, evil.

I bit my lip hard to keep back a biting remark. Blaming others for my own failure wasn't me.

"I shall leave now. Goodbye, Sofia, and if you ever change your mind about joining us, you know how to reach us." Devon's hand touched my shoulder lightly, then pulled back.

"I'll accompany you out," Thrain said, standing. My gaze followed him as he walked out a step behind Devon.

"You know you can't trust him," Aidan whispered as soon as the door closed. I nodded and shot him a smile. His expression remained serious, worried. "You can stay here for as long as you want."

"Thank you for the offer, but it's time to go home."

He hesitated. "As you wish. But if you ever need help, we'll be there for you. Amber and I will always be in your debt for saving Dallas."

My smile widened. "I appreciate it."

"I didn't take this job for the money," Kieran whispered. I opened my mouth to speak but he raised his hand, stopping me. " I don't know if you know about the Lore court." He trailed off, making it sound like a question. I shook my head so he continued, "Okay, I probably shouldn't tell you, but since only that blade can kill you I guess you're immortal too, sort of. Ever since Amber was turned into one of us, immortals from the Lore court have been after her, my brother and me. Gael was a member of the Lore court. He tried to get in touch with Aidan but couldn't get hold of him, so he made a deal with me. He said the Lore court would stop hunting us if I found the blade for him."

I could see the shame in his blue eyes. "Don't worry about it. I understand." I squeezed his hand to signal that I meant it.

"So we're good?" I nodded. A smile lit up Kieran's face. "You know, you're a gem. If Thrain and you didn't—" he clicked his tongue, making me blush, "—I would've taken you out to dinner, get a few drinks." His voice trailed off again.

"Kieran." Aidan's tone was sharp. A warning. Grinning, Kieran winked at me, and then we said goodbye, and he left with Aidan.

I stood up and walked to the window, minding my still aching ankle. The crow was there, peering at me from the sill. I opened the window and held out my hand gently to avoid startling the bird. But it wasn't shy. Cawing softly, it jumped on my arm, its claws pressing into my skin.

"You're a girl, aren't you?" I don't know what made me draw that conclusion, but it felt right. The crow cawed, whether to agree or negate my statement I couldn't tell.

"I'm sorry if you're not. And I'm really sorry for thinking you were the bad guy when all you wanted was to warn me," I whispered, smiling. "To my excuse I have to say my knowledge of human nature is crap."

The crow let out another caw before taking off into the sky. Maybe she was pissed off at me for assuming she didn't mean well. Or maybe she wasn't a girl after all. It didn't matter. What mattered was that I had fallen for Gael's lies and I wasn't proud of it. I should've seen behind his calculated mask and his fake friendliness. The signs had been there: his controlling behavior, his cold gazes when he thought I wasn't looking. My need for comfort after my sister's death had made me too trusting. It wouldn't happen again.

Thanks to a couple of painkillers, the pain in my chest had receded to a bearable throb. Engrossed in my thoughts, I took a shower and changed into my clothes, ready to go home. As much as I adored my new friends, all I wanted was a bit of solitude to plan my next step regarding my career because, yes, I wanted to be a star, but safety came first. And that needed lots of planning, which involved a home movement, a change in name and appearance so that Gael wouldn't find me straight away.

Dressed in my jeans and top, I sat down on the bed and took a deep breath to steady my sudden nervousness. What would be in store for me now?

How would my relationship with Thrain turn out away from all the turmoil and excitement?

A knock on the door and Thrain peered in. "Ready?"

I nodded and interlocked my fingers with his. We joined the others downstairs to say goodbye.

"You sure you don't want to stay a bit longer?" Amber whispered.

"I can't. College's starting soon and I have a million things to sort out first." I smiled and gave her a last squeeze. "See you again?"

"You bet." Her eyes sparkled with interest. "Do you think you'll enjoy college?"

Her strange question took me by surprise. I moistened my lips as I tried to make sense of it. "I hope so."

Aidan wrapped his arm around Amber's shoulders and pulled her close. "Want us to teleport you home?"

"Nah, we got that part covered," Thrain said.

"We'll miss you," Amber whispered, pushing a bundle into my hands. I peered at my passport and a few other things I thought I had left back in Rio.

"Thanks." I could feel moisture gathering in my eyes. Wiping my tears away, I let everyone give me one last hug and then accompanied Thrain to the car parked in the driveway. Thrain held the door open and I hopped in. As the vehicle pulled away, my resolve crumbled and the first two tears spilled down my cheeks. We drove through the open gates and down the winding country lane, past impenetrable

269

scrubland and thick trees with dark green leaves that filtered the sunlight. I leaned my head back, prepared for a long drive.

"I forgot to give you this," Thrain said, breaking the silence as he pulled out a red envelope from under his jacket.

"What is it?"

"Why don't you just open it?"

With shaking fingers I tore through the thick paper, cutting my finger in the process. Inside was a white card with gold cursive and lots of glitter. I began to read. "It's an invitation to Cass's birthday party," I said eventually.

Thrain's eyes twinkled as he winked at me. "You're officially one of us now, which means don't even think about coming up with an excuse for not attending because she won't have it. Knowing Cass, she'll bite your head off if you even try."

"I wouldn't even dream of it." Laughing, I pushed the envelope inside my handbag for safekeeping. "Are we going to the airport?"

"Nope."

"No?" I peered at his amused expression.

"Did you really think this is my usual means of transportation?" He pointed at the interior of the car. I didn't want to acknowledge that he was right in that I did assume that, so I shook my head.

"Obviously not. I knew you had a trick up your sleeve."

"It's not exactly a trick," Thrain said, slowing down until we moved at the speed of a snail. "More like an ability. Look ahead."

I peered at the empty air, wondering what I was supposed to see. And then I noticed the tiny particles sparkling a few feet away from us. They looked like sunlight catching in tiny dewdrops, and yet I knew dewdrops didn't hover in mid air.

"It's a portal," Thrain explained, stopping the car just a few inches away. "I have the ability to find and open them." The air around us started to crackle just a tiny bit, barely noticeable but enough to make the hair on my arms stand.

"So they're not everywhere?"

"There's plenty of exists, but only a few that can be entered. We usually drive around to find an entrance."

"And it can spit us out anywhere?"

"Only through an exit near a place of your choice." He shot me a grin. "Ready?"

"Wait!" I gripped the armrest tight and took a deep breath. "I'm ready."

Thrain hit the accelerator. A moment later, the car hit something hard, like the surface of water, catapulting us forward, then backward against our seats. Thrain laughed. I gasped, my heart skipping a beat. Dizziness washed over me and I closed my eyes. When I opened them a second later, our surrounding had changed from trees and lots of greenery to a dirty road near a bridge. My gaze wandered from the

271

passing vehicles whirling up dust to the skyscrapers in the distance. Manhattan lay on the other side of the river.

"We're in Brooklyn," Thrain said, switching lanes.

I nodded, already missing Scotland's breathtaking nature and clean air. "My apartment is around here."

"I know." Was that disappointment in his voice? I shot him a sideway glance. His face betrayed no emotion. Ten minutes later, I recognized my block. To my surprise, Thrain knew exactly where to park and get out. A hot hunk walking me to the door seemed surreal, as though I was coming back from an amazing adventure no one would ever believe. Only a few days ago, I had been nothing but a young woman trying to figure out who she was. I felt different now, more confident, more determined to embrace my true self.

Fishing in my handbag, I pulled out my keys with shaky fingers and tried to unlock the door to the building.

"Let me help you," Thrain said, grabbing the keys out of my hand. I let him do the work for me and followed him in through the narrow hall up to my apartment on the seventh floor. The hall still smelled of garbage as always, the plaster was still peeling off the wall in several places. I guessed I got used to it in the months I had been living here, but walking up with Thrain on my arm, the state of this place made me insecure. Would he think differently of me now the glamour was gone? What would he say to my tiny matchbox apartment with the old furniture I liked to call retro and the windows that wouldn't open most of the time?

"Want to come in?" I asked as soon as we reached the door, ready to find out the answers to all the questions bugging me.

He smiled. "I'd love to."

"My roommate might be here." I let him walk in and closed the door behind us.

"Then she'll get to watch quite a performance," Thrain whispered, catching me between the door and his hard body. I raised my lips to meet him as his arms wrapped around my waist. His hungry mouth descended onto mine, and for a moment the earth actually trembled beneath our feet.

Later, we lay on the couch, his arm draped around me, my fingers drawing circles on his naked chest where his tattoo seemed to twitch beneath my exploring fingers. I could see the silver thread around us, binding our souls together. It was strange looking at the sparkling air that seemed to be shifting slowly before my eyes, wondering whether he could see it too. My finger traced the air where the particles shimmered like tiny diamonds, barely visible if I didn't focus. We were bonded, drawn together by fate, which made the entire situation both bitter sweet and tragic. Two people from different worlds. Would it work out?

"Do you remember the talk you never wanted to have?" Thrain asked.

273

Groaning, I propped up on my elbow. What was it with this guy and his tendency to spoil the most beautiful moments with *talk*? I raised my brows. "Nope. Do you?"

"I can't stay here—with you."

His words caught me off guard. "You said that already."

"No, you don't understand." He shook his head, his eyes gleamed with something I couldn't pinpoint. "I want this. I want *us*, but it's going to be difficult with my job. I don't have a choice because I was made to serve. We'll have to figure something out because I'm not leaving you here all alone with a killer still on the loose."

His attitude pissed me off. As much as I fancied the idea of a proper, long-term boyfriend, I didn't like him thinking me weak. I wanted him to stay because he had fallen in love with me, but not to protect me. "I don't need a babysitter, Thrain." My tone sounded sharper than intended, and yet I couldn't help myself. I had been taking care of myself my whole life. Once I learned to use my new powers, I would be immortal, able to fend off even the Blade of Sorrow.

"Come with me." His thumb brushed my cheek gently, his green gaze betraying his emotions. It broke my heart to say it, and yet I had no choice.

"I want to, but I can't, just like you can't get away from your commitments." I took a deep breath to hide the quiver in my voice. "You see, a long time ago I made a promise to myself and to my family that I would succeed as a musician. I can't back down on my word."

He nodded. "Well, in that case I'm not going to try and change your mind. It wouldn't be right." He was putting my own needs before his. I appreciated his respect, but it stung that he didn't even try to find a solution to our dilemma.

"Thank you," I said, swallowing down my pride.

"I'll visit you whenever I can. We can take it from there," Thrain whispered.

Promise, I wanted to say, but I didn't because it would make me seem needy. I opened my mouth to say that I would very much like to see him again when my emotions choked me. So I just pressed my temple against his shoulder to hide the tears threatening to spill down my cheeks. I wished I had a choice, but I didn't. My voice was a gift I intended to use. My mother and grandmother were counting on me. I needed the money to help them out of poverty. I wouldn't disappoint them like my father did, not when they had sacrificed so much to get me where I was now.

An hour later, Thrain left me with a last kiss and the promise to return soon. I knew soon could mean anything. A day. A week. A month. A long time when surviving even an hour without him already seemed like the toughest task of my life.

Epilogue

Six weeks later

The sun spilled bright rays through the café window, where I worked during my study breaks and the regular, badly paid performances my band mate, Aaron, set me up with. We were still a team, albeit a more efficient one now that Gael was no longer here to monitor my every move. With experience, my voice had gained in depth, and with every gig I felt more confident. Aaron said if we kept up the exposure we'd be a household name soon. I trusted his knowledge of the business, so I focused on using every opportunity to perform while staying away from the usual industry parties fueled with sex and drugs.

In the last six weeks, my inspiration had been at an all time high. I had been missing Thrain so much that I poured everything I had into songwriting. Like promised, he had called but our conversations had been brief and superficial. Several times I wanted to ask when I'd be seeing him again, but I chickened out. The only glimpse I caught of him was at Cass's birthday party, followed by a heated kiss and yet another painful goodbye. He hadn't called in a week now, which made me wonder what he was up to and whether he had already forgotten about me.

I wiped the counter to finish my morning shift, then hurried home to get changed for my first class. A few days ago, I had moved into a room on campus, figuring I was closer to college and could fully focus on my studies. Besides, I would be safer here. My new roommate would arrive today, so I made a quick stop at a convenience store to get coffee and cake. A good first impression could decide whether sharing a room with a stranger for the next four years would be bearable or pure hell.

As I opened the door to the dorm room, the bathroom lights were already switched on.

"Hello?" My voice reverberated from the walls, making me cringe because it sounded so insecure. Truth was, I wasn't over the fact that Gael had tried to kill me.

A girl dressed in jeans and a long sweater, black hair in a ponytail, appeared in the doorway and held out her hand. "Oh, hi. You must be Sofia. I'm Liz, your new roommate." She was pretty with tiny freckles covering her cheeks, a bit taller and more athletic, but she didn't look like she was the chocolate-skipping kind. I instantly warmed up to her.

Grabbing her hand in a tight grip, I looked behind her at the things cluttering the bathroom floor, then back to her. "Sorry about the mess. I didn't expect you before   eight."

She nodded, her eyes shimmering. "Yeah. I hope you don't mind."

"Not at all."

She grinned and something flickered in her gaze. I thought I recognized her from somewhere, but it couldn't be. I had never met her before.

"So we'll be roommates, huh? How cool is that?" She pointed at the box in my hand. "Is that cake?"

I smiled. "Chocolate topping. Figured you'd like it."

"Love it. I got you a gift as well," Liz whispered, her tone growing a little husky.

"Really?" I raised my brows at her broad smile and her sparkling eyes. There was something weird about her. She was staring at me strangely, like something was wrong with me. It freaked me out a bit.

"It's on your nightstand."

I nodded and walked past her through the tiny hall into our bedroom. It was quite spacious with two beds and desks as well as a tiny walk-in closet and a few bookshelves. What I liked best, however, was the view on the communal garden that I knew I would frequent often. As soon my gaze fell on the huge, hideous thing on my bed, my heart almost stopped and I let out a loud shriek. There, right next to pillow sat a butt-ugly gargoyle with shiny, red eyes peering

278

right at me. Its mouth hung slightly open, revealing a long string of sharp teeth. I swear for a moment I thought it grinned at me, but it might as well been a silent growl. Either way, this thing looked very much alive—I could tell from the way its ginormous head cocked to one side to get a better glimpse of me, probably considering whether to have me for lunch now or a bit later. I took a step back, unsure whether to dash for the door in case it might give chase.

Something touched my shoulder gently, startling me. I turned sharply and peered into the most gorgeous green eyes ever. "You don't like your gift?" Thrain asked with a grin playing on his full lips. Lips I wanted to kiss that instant.

"You scared the hell out of me," I said, catching my breath. "How did you get in here?"

He wrapped his arms around my waist and pulled me close until our lips met. "I have a few tricks up my sleeve."

"My roommate might not like it." I peered behind him, where Liz had just been standing a minute ago. The hall to our en suite stood empty. "Where did she—" My gaze wandered back to him, regarding him, his gorgeous smile, the way he carried himself, so confident, amused, mischievous. Something flickered in his eyes, reminding me that I had seen it before. I could feel my brain working, putting together the missing pieces of the puzzle. Thrain was a demon, but what did he say he could do? Tracking and shape

279

shifting. Realization kicked in when I remembered the girl in the woods on the day Gael tried to kill me. She had been the spitting image of me. Later, while Gael kept me hostage inside the circle, Thrain had been standing in the girl's place, next to Devon. Thrain had tried to fool Gael in order to save me.

"You're my roommate," I said, not trying to hide the surprise in my voice.

Thrain's grin widened. "I thought you'd never figure it out."

"So, are you staying?"

"For as long as I can." He moistened his lips as he drew me down on the bed. I settled into his arms, inhaling his manly scent, as I tried to ignore the gargoyle inching closer to sniff my hand. "Since you saved Cass, the big boss has decided to give me a bit more free time. I'll have to leave every now and then, during which Bonnie—" Thrain pointed at the gargoyle "—will be taking care of you."

Bonnie? He couldn't be serious. More like Monster or Craze. The gargoyle grunted and slumped down on the bed, snuggling next to my thigh like a cuddly cat. I wasn't sure whether to rub her head or run away, screaming. I figured it might take me a while to warm up to my new pet. Particularly at night.

"Guys aren't allowed to spend the night," I said.

Thrain nodded. "Which is why I'm going to be Liz most of the time."

The thought almost made me burst out with laughter. "You want me to make out with a *girl*?"

"You would do that?" Thrain cocked a brow.

I slapped his arm. "Just so you know the rules. First, no touching when you're Liz."

"Come on, admit it. You thought I was hot."

He couldn't be serious. I slapped his arm again, this time harder. "I mean it. Second, I'm not cleaning after you. And third—" I took a deep breath to steady my racing heart "—I'm not going to bed without a goodnight kiss *every* night."

"Rule number three is definitely a must," Thrain whispered, cupping my face in his hands. "Unless you have other plans, I hope you don't mind we start practicing now?"

I shook my head then pulled him down to kiss him, my first class of the day forgotten.

THE END... —FOR NOW